# Where's Olivia?

## A Calico Cat Mystery

## Patricia Fry

# Where's Olivia?

## A Calico Cat Mystery
## by Patricia Fry

copyright © 2021 Patricia Fry

ISBN 978-1-7369430-4-5

Cover Art: Bernadette E. Kazmarski

Cover layout: Dennis Mullican
Page layout: Dennis Mullican

Printed in U.S.A. by: KDP

"Come on, Olivia," Parker complained, moving things around on the shelves in the pantry, but she didn't see anything resembling a calico cat. Becoming more frustrated, she called, "Olivia! Darn it, where are you?" *Under the bed,* she thought, turning around and almost stumbling over the very cat she was searching for.

"Olivia," Parker huffed, "you've done that sneaky materializing thing again." She stared down at the cat, who sat innocently looking up at her from the middle of the kitchen floor, and tried not to laugh. "How you do that, Olivia, I'll never know. Where were you, you little scamp?" She picked up the fluffy cat and cooed, "Don't you know I worry when I can't find you? You're an awfully good girl, but you can sure drive me bonkers when you hide like that."

Parker fastened a harness around Olivia and snapped the leash to it. She picked up her jacket, purse, and a tote bag filled mostly with things Olivia might need and an extra sweater for herself. "Let's go," she said, leading Olivia out the front door to her car. Once she had secured the cat into her car seat and pulled out onto the roadway, she glanced at the dashboard clock. "Darn it, we're going to be late. The detective is probably waiting for us." Parker ran her hand over Olivia's silky coat as the cat sat up in her car seat, and she explained, "He wants to discuss strategy—you know, for getting his daughter back. I hope we can find Hannah and bring

# Where's Olivia?

## A Calico Cat Mystery

## Book Two

"Olivia! Olivia, where are you now?" Parker Campbell called as she removed the items she thought she'd need for the day from her larger purse and organized them into a smaller one. "We're meeting the detective for another briefing. You don't want to be left behind, do you, Olivia?" When the calico cat did not appear Parker gazed down the hallway, glanced into the kitchen, and quickly scanned the living room again. "Olivia, I'm not in the mood to play hide-and-seek with you, especially when you don't play fair."

She remembered something and trotted into the bedroom. "Are you still sleeping all scrunched up in that shoebox?" Parker opened the closet door and said to herself, "Not there. I didn't close you in a drawer again, did I?" She began pulling out dresser drawers and peering inside, musing, *Actually, I don't think I've opened a drawer since I got dressed.* She frowned. *But I did open the pantry to put the coffee away.* She went to the kitchen.

her home before Houston rolls into town. I'd sure like to spend some time with him without having to worry about work. I have a pretty good start on that article featuring the city's oldest cat colony, and that's a good thing, because it looks like I'll have at least two more article assignments after that one."

When Olivia let out one of her high-pitched mews Parker smiled. "Yes, I'm sure I'll have a request for a piece on that awful mudslide tragedy the feral cats discovered, and there's surely a story behind Hannah's disappearance." She ran her hand over Olivia's fur again. "Now we need to focus our time and energy on helping the detective find her. I want you to be extra alert, now, and aware. Got your big-girl pantaloons on?" She laughed at the vision.

Parker was quiet for several minutes, then she said, "You know, Olivia, people might think I'm crazy for having these conversations with you, but it's helpful to me. That's how I think things through." She responded to another squeaky mew. "That's right. When I hold the thoughts in my head they just keep rolling around and around, but if I write them down or verbalize them, it helps me to—you know—sort through them, organize them, and figure out how to deal with them. You, my love-love, are a real help in that way, and I appreciate it." More sternly she said, "What I don't appreciate is when you hide from me." She giggled. "Maybe you're just getting tired of my chatter. Is that it? You need your personal space to do your own pondering?" She ruffled the fur on Olivia's head. "Well, my sweet girl, get used to my prattle because that's the way I roll." She chuckled. "I suppose if you could talk you'd be telling me to get used to your penchant for hiding because that's the way *you* roll."

Parker sat up straighter and scanned the restaurant parking lot as she pulled in. "Yup, there's the detective's car. I hope he hasn't been waiting for too long." She parked her Jeep SUV, then unfastened Olivia's car-seat restraint and urged her to jump out of it. "Oops," she yelped when she opened the car door. "It's going to be chilly on the patio. You wait there, Olivia, while I put on my jacket. I hope he found us a table near one of those heaters." She grabbed her purse and tote, then picked up Olivia. "Come on, sweetie. Let's go see what Mr. Jud has in mind for us today."

"Did you sleep in?" Detective Judson Caldwell asked when Parker approached with Olivia. He greeted the cat. "Hi there, fluffy girl. May I order you a saucer of cream?"

Parker was quick to say, "No." She explained, "Milk, and especially cream, upsets her tummy. She's okay. I brought her kibbles in case she gets hungry or cranky." She took a small cat bed from the tote and laid it next to her chair, murmuring, "In the off chance that you get sleepy, Olivia."

4

He leaned forward with his elbows on the table. "Okay, while you were gone I went down some of the standard avenues one would take to locate a missing person—you know, to eliminate all the worries—the morgue, hospitals…"

"How morbid," Parker said, frowning. "Is this the first time you've done that? You didn't do that when you first knew Hannah was missing?"

"Yes," he cranked. "Of course I did, but since we have new information I felt it needed to be done again. Things can change after seven years. She could have eventually walked out into the open." He took a breath. "I checked for arrests—the whole gamut. Nothing. Hannah Caldwell still does not show up anywhere on anyone's radar."

"What about the human remains?" Parker asked quietly.

"Those we found out at the cat colony?" he asked. "Yeah, I'm waiting for test results. That could take a while, you know—figuring out all of the jumbled mess of evidence and body parts we found in that mudslide. The fact that it happened over seven years ago makes it even more difficult. Yeah, I think we're beyond that as a solution to finding Hannah. Remember, the call she made to my wife's phone came in *after* the slide occurred. The only way she could have ended up in that death pit with those ten or so other people is if someone…" he choked up. "It's painful to even think about, but it's gotta be considered." He took a

7

deep breath and continued, "Those people she was with could have taken her back there and buried her or something. But why would they do that? No," he said with conviction, "I believe she's alive. I just don't understand why she hasn't called me. Has she gone away and started a new life somewhere? Does someone have her—are they holding her captive? Is she being drugged and can't get away? I'm telling you, she's a resourceful girl…" he paused, "…well, woman." He lowered his head. "She's twenty-six now. I lost out on seven years of her life. Hell, she could have a kid or several kids by now, but why is she staying away? Why for this long? I need answers, and I need them soon."

"Okay," Parker said calmly, "so there's nothing new since our jaunt out to the address you had—the one that Olivia found in Hannah's closet, right?"

"Yeah, in Hannah's secret hiding place," he mused.

Parker checked on Olivia while considering Jud's words. "It appeared from the note she left that she had met the people she was with before the night of the mudslide, and she must have had some reservations about them."

He nodded. "Yes, she was—I mean she *is* intuitive that way. I agree that she had a bad feeling about those people, or she wouldn't have left a note with their address on it, then placed a call to let us know she'd hidden it." He slumped in his her home before Houston rolls into town. I'd sure like to spend some time with him without having to worry about work. I have a pretty good start on that article featuring the city's oldest cat colony, and that's a good thing, because it looks like I'll have at least two more article assignments after that one."

When Olivia let out one of her high-pitched mews Parker smiled. "Yes, I'm sure I'll have a request for a piece on that awful mudslide tragedy the feral cats discovered, and there's surely a story behind Hannah's disappearance." She ran her hand over Olivia's fur again. "Now we need to focus our time and energy on helping the detective find her. I want you to be extra alert, now, and aware. Got your big-girl pantaloons on?" She laughed at the vision.

Parker was quiet for several minutes, then she said, "You know, Olivia, people might think I'm crazy for having these conversations with you, but it's helpful to me. That's how I think things through." She responded to another squeaky mew. "That's right. When I hold the thoughts in my head they just keep rolling around and around, but if I write them down or verbalize them, it helps me to—you know—sort through them, organize them, and figure out how to deal with them. You, my love-love, are a real help in that way, and I appreciate it." More sternly she said, "What I don't appreciate is when you hide from me." She giggled. "Maybe you're just getting tired of my chatter. Is that it? You need your personal space to do your own

3

pondering?" She ruffled the fur on Olivia's head. "Well, my sweet girl, get used to my prattle because that's the way I roll." She chuckled. "I suppose if you could talk you'd be telling me to get used to your penchant for hiding because that's the way *you* roll."

Parker sat up straighter and scanned the restaurant parking lot as she pulled in. "Yup, there's the detective's car. I hope he hasn't been waiting for too long." She parked her Jeep SUV, then unfastened Olivia's car-seat restraint and urged her to jump out of it. "Oops," she yelped when she opened the car door. "It's going to be chilly on the patio. You wait there, Olivia, while I put on my jacket. I hope he found us a table near one of those heaters." She grabbed her purse and tote, then picked up Olivia. "Come on, sweetie. Let's go see what Mr. Jud has in mind for us today."

"Did you sleep in?" Detective Judson Caldwell asked when Parker approached with Olivia. He greeted the cat. "Hi there, fluffy girl. May I order you a saucer of cream?"

Parker was quick to say, "No." She explained, "Milk, and especially cream, upsets her tummy. She's okay. I brought her kibbles in case she gets hungry or cranky." She took a small cat bed from the tote and laid it next to her chair, murmuring, "In the off chance that you get sleepy, Olivia."

4

The detective laughed. "It appears she'd rather sit at the table with us. Look at her—she just jumped right up into that chair."

Parker cringed. "Yes, I'm afraid that's my fault."

"Of course it is," he grumbled. "You spoil her."

"But she has good table manners," she countered. Parker glanced around. "I doubt they'd appreciate seeing a cat sitting at a table out here on the patio, though." She picked up Olivia and placed her in her bed, then scooted the empty chair up against the table.

The crafty calico leaped from her bed and into the chair again. When Olivia couldn't sit up and see across the table, she simply lay down in the seat and watched the activity from there. Parker smiled at the cat and ran her hand over her fur, then asked the detective, "So what's new? Have you learned anything more about your daughter's whereabouts?" She winced. "By the way, I'm sorry I had to run off like I did day before yesterday. A friend desperately needed my help." She patted his arm. "Well, you know Savannah and Rags. They helped us with the cat colony fiasco."

He nodded. "Yes. Nice gal, and what a cat!" He tilted his head. "They needed help?"

"Yes." Parker thought for a moment, then said, "I'll tell you about it sometime. It was quite a frightening situation." She shook her head as if to erase the images and asked, "So, what did I miss yesterday?"

The detective handed Parker a menu and suggested, "Let's order, then I'll fill you in."

After they placed their orders Parker watched the server walk away, then said to Jud, "Okay, catch me up to speed. Have you learned anything more since we talked last?"

"Yes," he said. "I'm glad you're back." He paused, then added, "And the cat."

"You're glad to see Olivia?" she asked. "That's surprising. You usually…"

"I like cats," he said, defensively. "What makes you think I wouldn't be glad to see her or that I don't like her or something?"

Parker grinned impishly. "You don't approve of her sitting at the table with us."

"Yeah, well, that's because she's a cat. Some of you cat people don't seem to get that—a cat is a cat."

"Until you need a cat like Olivia or Rags to do something out of the ordinary, right?" she challenged.

"How'd you know I wanted to use her?" he asked.

"Well, Jud," Parker said, "I haven't known you for long, but I think I know you pretty well—at least some aspects of who you are." She asked more quietly, "What do you want her to do?"

6

He leaned forward with his elbows on the table. "Okay, while you were gone I went down some of the standard avenues one would take to locate a missing person—you know, to eliminate all the worries—the morgue, hospitals…"

"How morbid," Parker said, frowning. "Is this the first time you've done that? You didn't do that when you first knew Hannah was missing?"

"Yes," he cranked. "Of course I did, but since we have new information I felt it needed to be done again. Things can change after seven years. She could have eventually walked out into the open." He took a breath. "I checked for arrests—the whole gamut. Nothing. Hannah Caldwell still does not show up anywhere on anyone's radar."

"What about the human remains?" Parker asked quietly.

"Those we found out at the cat colony?" he asked. "Yeah, I'm waiting for test results. That could take a while, you know—figuring out all of the jumbled mess of evidence and body parts we found in that mudslide. The fact that it happened over seven years ago makes it even more difficult. Yeah, I think we're beyond that as a solution to finding Hannah. Remember, the call she made to my wife's phone came in *after* the slide occurred. The only way she could have ended up in that death pit with those ten or so other people is if someone…" he choked up. "It's painful to even think about, but it's gotta be considered." He took a deep breath and continued, "Those people she was with could have taken her back there and buried her or something. But why would they do that? No," he said with conviction, "I believe she's alive. I just don't understand why she hasn't called me. Has she gone away and started a new life somewhere? Does someone have her—are they holding her captive? Is she being drugged and can't get away? I'm telling you, she's a resourceful girl…" he paused, "…well, woman." He lowered his head. "She's twenty-six now. I lost out on seven years of her life. Hell, she could have a kid or several kids by now, but why is she staying away? Why for this long? I need answers, and I need them soon."

"Okay," Parker said calmly, "so there's nothing new since our jaunt out to the address you had—the one that Olivia found in Hannah's closet, right?"

"Yeah, in Hannah's secret hiding place," he mused.

Parker checked on Olivia while considering Jud's words. "It appeared from the note she left that she had met the people she was with before the night of the mudslide, and she must have had some reservations about them."

He nodded. "Yes, she was—I mean she *is* intuitive that way. I agree that she had a bad feeling about those people, or she wouldn't have left a note with their address on it, then placed a call to let us know she'd hidden it." He slumped in his chair. "She's probably wondering why her daddy didn't come to her rescue. If only I'd listened to my wife's phone messages before this. She was too sick to care about phone calls, and I was too shook up and confused to even look at her phone. That was the last thing on my mind. Hell, I sure wasn't in the mood to listen to frivolous calls from her friends and her annoying sister. All those years I've wondered where Hannah was, and all along the answer was in that damn phone. Now it might be too late, like seven years too late."

"Maybe not," Parker said. "Maybe not." But her thoughts didn't match her words. She, too, was worried about what they would learn as they continued their investigation. *Why hasn't Hannah contacted her dad by now?* she wondered. *Maybe it was because he and his wife didn't respond to the message she left. Maybe she just went on with her life. Let's hope that's the case, because the potential alternatives are frightful.*

Once their breakfast was served, Jud looked at Parker's plate. "Are you on a diet?"

She chuckled. "I could ask you the same thing. One poached egg on an English muffin?"

"And fruit," he said, motioning toward a small bowl filled with grapes, pineapple, and a variety of melon. He admitted. "My stomach doesn't take kindly to large portions lately. At this rate I'll soon need suspenders to hold up my pants like my Uncle George did." He took a few bites and another swig of coffee, then said, "I found out one thing that I think is important."

"What?" she asked, scooping her egg onto a half slice of toast and breaking the yolk.

Before he could respond, a woman walked up to their table. "Excuse me," she said, "I'm Glenda. My friend and I are having the best time over there." She giggled. "You see, my junior-high-school friend, Sylvia and I get together a couple of times a year and catch up with each other while adventuring." She laughed. "We've been adventuring almost every year for nearly five decades."

"Adventuring?" Parker repeated, amused.

Glenda nodded excitedly. "Wherever we go together, things happen. Adventures pop up out of nowhere. Today, we were most fascinated to see a cat dining out."

Parker glanced down at the chair where Olivia had been lying and suddenly felt a rush of panic. "Olivia!" she called. She scooted her chair back and looked around under the table.

Glenda was quick to say, "She's okay." She pointed. "Sylvia's sharing her scrambled egg with her. Olivia, huh? She sure is a beauty." She snickered. "And evidently a might sneaky. You didn't see her slink away?"

Parker shook her head and stood up. "I sure didn't, but you're right, she *is* sneaky that way. Gosh, I'm sorry."

"No worries," Glenda said. "We're both cat lovers, and Miss Olivia has created such a bright spot in our first day together on this trip."

"How long has she…" Parker started, walking across the patio with Glenda.

"Long enough for us to fall in love with her," Glenda said giddily. "We're getting ready to leave now. We have a tour bus to catch, so I thought I'd better blow her cover and let you know where she had wandered off to."

"Dang," Parker said, approaching Sylvia and Olivia. "I wish she wouldn't do that. I mean how…?"

Sylvia laughed. "She's a darling." She picked her up and held her against her face. "A devious diva. I saw how it happened. When you pushed the chair in so she couldn't get on your table, the leash came out from under the chair leg." Dramatically she added, "As soon as you weren't looking, here she came." She giggled. "What a thrill." She handed the cat to Parker. "Thank you for sharing her. She's wonderful."

"Well, you're welcome," Parker said, smiling into Olivia's face as she held her. "I'm glad she behaved herself. Thank you for entertaining her."

"Certainly," Glenda said. She ran her hand over Olivia's fur. "It was our pleasure."

Parker started to walk away with Olivia, then stopped. "Would you like me to take a picture of the two of you with her?" She chuckled. "You might want it for your photo album of adventures."

"Would you?" Glenda asked, handing Parker her phone. She reached for Olivia and sat down next to Sylvia, holding the cat between them. "This is great!" she said, before releasing Olivia to Parker and taking her phone back. She waved as Parker walked away. "Good bye, Olivia. Thank you for making our morning."

When Parker returned to their table with Olivia, Jud shook his head. "Unbelievable. There's never a dull moment when you travel with a cat, is there? It's kind of like having a mischievous child with you."

"Pretty much," Parker agreed. She poured water into Olivia's cat bowl and secured the cat near it, then she continued eating her breakfast. She looked up at Jud and prompted, "So you learned something new while I was gone?"

"Yes, we actually drove past the wrong house the other day when we were scoping out the area and gathering information."

"We did?" she asked, surprised. "That was the address we found in Hannah's hidey-hole, wasn't it? Although it was kind of scribbled, so I guess we could have read it wrong."

"We might have," Jud said. "I did more snooping while you were gone and found out that isn't where those kids Hannah named—you know, Brad and Travis—that isn't where they lived. The house—an old Victorian home—where they used to live is now some sort of a business. That's what they're doing with the Victorian homes in the area—turning them into businesses."

"It was the wrong address? Where is it? What sort of a business?" she asked.

"Well, it's on North Lake Drive," Jud said. "The address where you and I went is on South Lake Drive."

"So did you go inside the one on North Lake Drive," she asked, "the one that's now a business?"

He shook his head. "It wasn't all that inviting."

She frowned. "What do you mean? What sort of invitation do you need to walk into a business?"

"Well, it's not like it's a sporting goods store or an ice cream parlor where you can enter and look around without being noticed," he explained. "This place is more resort-like. No, I didn't go inside. I wanted to wait for you, but I did ask a few questions. The attendant at that gas station on the edge of town was minimally helpful. He said that group who lived there before the remodel, when the place was all rundown, used to come into the minimart fairly often until around three years ago when the old house was taken over by relatives and turned into some sort of dance studio-slash-spa. He thinks it's a dance studio and maybe a spa, although there is no signage around the place indicating that."

"So these were Brad's or Travis's relatives?" she asked.

"I guess," he said.

"And the gas station guy didn't know where those two boys went?" Parker asked. Before Jud could respond, she asked another question. "Did he ever see Hannah with them?"

"No—well, maybe. He couldn't be sure. He said the boys were often in the company of young women, but he didn't pay much attention to them. I guess they didn't stand out."

"Well, from that picture you carry of your daughter," Parker said, "she is a standout. She appears quite vivacious. What did he mean by saying she didn't stand out?"

"I don't know," Jud said. "The guy sort of shut down on me, like he didn't want to talk about the family or the place. He said that my picture of Hannah did not look familiar to him." Jud leaned back in his chair and stretched, then said, "I guess I don't have anything much new to go on, so we still have a lot of work to do." He pushed his plate aside, laid a pad on the table, and began flipping through the pages, reciting, "Hannah was last seen seven years ago on January sixteenth, and last heard from the following day on January seventeenth—you know, when she called my wife's phone. She was thought to be with at least two dudes named Brad and Travis, who reportedly lived at that address on North Lake Drive. Seven years later, the address is

14

a dance studio-slash-spa. County records show that the old Victorian home was turned into a two-family dwelling about thirty years ago—you know, like a duplex. Three years ago is when they did the major remodel of the entire property, and that seems to be when the young people left." He looked across the table at Parker. "What?"

"What do you mean, *what*?" she asked.

He explained, "I saw you jump to attention. You have an idea or a thought, unless the cat bit your toe under the table or something."

"Yes," she said. "I was just wondering if we could speak with the contractor who did the renovation from duplex to dance studio. Maybe Hannah left a clue in the floor or walls like she did in her closet at your house." Before he could respond, she added, "We need to speak with neighbors. Someone who still lives in that area will probably remember Brad and Travis. They might have seen Hannah and even talked to her. We need to track down people who lived in that neighborhood five, six, seven years ago, and we need to find out Brad's and Travis's last names. Can we maybe get some of that from Hannah's friends—the friends she hung out with before she disappeared? You said she was a student at a community college. What about teachers and classmates? Did she have a job, do volunteer work? Have you logged that sort of information in your notes there?"

Jud took a swig of coffee and stared at Parker over his mug for a moment, finally saying, "Man, are you a house afire. He made a line of checks on his tablet, saying, "Yes, Yes, Yes, and Yes. Are you ready to go? I'd like to get back in the groove with this thing while you're hot." He stood up, tossed some money onto the table, and looked down at Olivia. "Ready to go, pussycat?"

"So where do you want to start?" Parker asked, slipping into Jud's car with Olivia.

He grinned. "Like you said, neighbors. I've already talked briefly to a few of them. I'd like to continue with that until I have a broader picture of who it is we're dealing with." When he sensed that Parker was looking at him, he explained, "I'd like to have more background information on that family, especially those two boys, before we barge in." He glanced at his watch. "We have a meeting with a woman who lived in the neighborhood for most of her life until around four years ago when she moved into The Victorian Assisted Living Home. Then I want to talk to a realtor who also manages some of the properties in the area—a Mr. Atkinson. I saw his *for sale* sign in front of a couple of houses and contacted him. We have an appointment with him later this morning."

"Did he manage the property where Brad and Travis lived?" Parker asked. When Jud glanced at her, she explained, "Hey, if I had young people living in my house, even if they were related and maybe *especially* if they were related, I'd be hiring a property manager to take care of the problems, because with young people living there, you're going to have problems."

"I hear you," Jud quipped. "Yeah, I don't think that property was under Mr. Atkinson's scrutiny, but maybe."

"You've already done quite a bit of research," Parker said, "and you have a plan of action."

He nodded. "Yes I do. Once we work phase one of the plan, we'll start knocking on doors to see if anyone else knows anything."

She faced him. "If you're so organized and you have all these leads, why do you need me? I could have stayed home and worked on my writing projects. I need to finish up the cat colony story and get that thing submitted. The cat ladies are eager for the publicity, you know. They hope someone will read the piece and come forward with an offer of land for the feral cats or maybe money to build a safe outdoor space for them. I'd really like to get their story out sooner rather than later."

"Do you want me to take you home?" he blurted.

"And leave you to conduct those interviews on your own?" she said, grinning. "No, I think I'd better tag along to keep you from…"

"From what?" he growled.

"Well, from letting your emotions get in the way," she said more gently.

Neither of them spoke for a few minutes until Jud announced, "Here we are. Mrs. Knudson is in room two thirty-five, unless she's participating in one of the activities in the day room or working out at the gym or taking a stroll around the grounds." He took a breath. "We'll check at the front desk."

"Wow!" Parker said. "It sounds like quite a facility, and she must be one active woman. How old is she?"

"She'll be ninety-six next month and proud of it." He chuckled. "Oh, and she does a lot of phone-chatting. She says she stays in touch with family and friends almost daily on her cell phone."

"So you've already talked to her? How did you find her?" Parker asked.

"I snooped around—you know, inquired at some of the local businesses." He pulled into a parking space. "Mrs. Knudson was kind of a mainstay in the neighborhood. Her house is one of the oldest in that area." When he saw Parker pick up Olivia he asked, "You aren't taking the cat, are you? I'm not sure they allow animals inside there."

"Well, I'm not leaving her in the car," Parker insisted. "I never leave her in the car. Olivia goes where I go." She waved a hand dismissively. "Besides, well-behaved animals are usually welcome in assisted-living facilities and even hospitals. Volunteers often bring in kittens and puppies to visit the residents in these places. Animals are therapeutic. And, in case you didn't know," she said, facing him, "Olivia is a registered therapy cat. If they refuse admittance to her, I'll show them her certification."

Jud simply stared at her and shook his head. "Well, come on, Parker and Olivia the healer."

"Heeler?" Parker questioned. "She's not very good at heeling like a trained dog."

He laughed and explained, "No, healer— H-E-A-L." Jud greeted a woman who sat behind a large counter typing on an ergonomic keyboard. "Hello, we're here to see Mrs. Knudson, Virginia Knudson."

The woman glanced up, then took a second look at Olivia, who was in Parker's arms. She smiled brightly. "What a pretty cat. Is she a therapy cat? Did you bring her to share with our residents?"

"Um…" Parker stammered. "Not really. We'd just like to visit with Mrs. Knudson today. I believe we have an appointment with her."

The woman nodded. "Yes, but she didn't tell me that one of her visitors would be such a beautiful cat." The woman reached out a hand to Parker, then to Jud. "By the way, I'm Katherine, the activities director here. Do you know Mrs. Knudson? She does love the activities. She rarely misses one unless a phone call comes in from her son or daughters or one of her grandchildren. So what time is your appointment," she glanced at her watch, "ten?"

Jud nodded, and Katherine picked up the phone. "Let me check with her floor assistant to see where she is and if she's ready for visitors."

"May I ask," Jud said quietly, "is she—you know—with it?" He added, "When I spoke with her yesterday she seemed pretty clear-minded."

Katherine studied his face for a moment, then laughed. "Do you mean cognizant? Oh yes. She doesn't miss a beat, that one." She placed a phone call, then said, "She's in her room waiting for your arrival. I hope you like tea. She always serves hot tea to her guests."

Parker smiled. "Does she get many guests?"

"At times, yes, but for most people in their nineties, unless they have family or they've remained in the workplace for many years and made some younger friends, there's no one left to visit them."

"I never thought about that," Parker said, frowning. "That would be rather lonely, wouldn't it?"

"Most of us *don't* think about things like that until we get to that age or spend time with someone who is." Katherine smiled. "I'm sure you'll hear all about it from Virginia." She ran her hand over Olivia's fur. "She will adore meeting this cutie. Virginia's probably our most avid cat lady." She chuckled. "There's a group that occasionally brings kittens here for an enrichment activity, and there's often a kitten missing at the end of their visit."

"Really?" Parker said.

Katherine nodded. "But we all know where to look for it. When we find Virginia, we have to pry the little thing from her fingers." She grinned. "Beware that she doesn't pocket your pretty girl." Before Parker could respond, Katherine said, "Room two thirty-five." She pointed. "Take the elevator to the next level."

"Thank you," Parker said, following Jud with Olivia in her arms.

"Certainly," Katherine called. "Have a good visit, folks."

Once they were in the elevator, Jud tickled Olivia's head. "Did you hear that, pussycat? The nice lady might want to keep you. Would you like to live here? Looks like a pretty nice place, actually."

"Sure does," Parker said. She snuggled with Olivia. "But you're going home with me, sweet britches."

Both Jud and Parker chuckled when Olivia looked up at her and mewed in her high-pitched voice.

"What was that?" Jud asked. "Sounded to me like a protest."

Parker smirked at him playfully, then stepped out of the elevator. "There it is," she said, leading the way.

Jud caught up to her, and he knocked lightly on the door.

It wasn't long before they heard a cheery voice. "Coming. I'll be right there." Virginia Knudson opened the door, smiled, and asked, "Mr. Caldwell, I presume?"

He nodded. "Yes, and this is Parker Campbell and her cat."

"A kitty-cat," she trilled. She motioned for the pair to enter the living room saying, "I didn't know you were bringing me a kitty-cat. No one told me that. What a sweet surprise. Is she for keeps?" she asked, closing the door. Before Parker could respond, the woman reached for Olivia, then stopped and asked, "What are all those straps? Why do you have her tied up like that? Has she been a naughty girl?" She grinned. "Are you surprised that I know she's a girl without even looking? Well, I know cats. I know that she's a female because of her coloring. In all of my years of loving and caring for cats, I've never seen a male calico. Tri-colored cats—calicos and torties—are just about always female." She added, "I can also sometimes tell the gender of a cat just by looking into its little face." She clasped her hands together in delight. "Look at that kitty face. She is so dear." Virginia tugged at the harness and asked again, "Why do you have her tied up like that?"

Parker smiled. "This is Olivia. She travels with me, and she wears a halter and a leash for her safety."

"She even has a special car seat for the cat," Jud added.

The woman looked at him, then back at Olivia. "My, my," she murmured. "And the cat tolerates it? All the cats I've known were free spirits, you know."

When Virginia seemed to be having a moment with her memories Parker suggested, "Mrs. Knudson, how about if I take the harness off her, and you can hold her on your lap? Would you like that?"

"Yes," the woman said, giddily. "Yes, very much." She glanced toward the kitchenette. "But first let me get you a cup of tea. I make the best tea in the building—maybe in the neighborhood and even the state. I almost opened a teahouse, you know, after I retired from nursing."

"What stopped you?" Parker asked. She removed Olivia's harness, then picked up the cat and cradled her in her arms.

"Oh, I don't know," Virginia said, "I think because I was so busy. I belonged to clubs and groups, and I did a lot of traveling all over the place to stay close to my family." She asked, "Ms. Parker, do you have children?" Before Parker could answer, she said sternly, "Make sure to send them to a good college, because they're going to meet girls or guys from other states or countries, marry, and move to their spouse's hometown. Only one of my three children still lives in California, and he's clear down in San Diego. Don't you know I've had a marvelous time traveling all over the United States to be with my children and grandchildren? It was wonderful while it lasted." She sighed deeply and admitted, "I sure miss seeing them now, though, since I'm no longer traveling. I guess it's a double-edged sword—you know, the decision to send your children off to a good university."

"I'll remember that," Parker said.

"Okay, where was I?" Virginia asked. "Oh yes, tea. It's tea time. You will have tea with me, won't you?"

Parker and Jud both nodded, and Parker said, "I'd love it. What kind are you making today?"

As if she were sharing a secret, the woman said, "Lavender-ginger. It's one of my favorites."

"Sounds lovely," Parker said. When Olivia began to squirm in her arms, she held on to her, crooning, "No tea for you, love-love. You just settle down, now."

"Love-love," Virginia repeated. "I adore that. Love-love. What a great pet name." She peered into Parker's face. "You really do love her, don't you? That's how I felt about some of my special kitty-cats. They're all wonderful, but some of them—well, there's just a deeper connection. Do you know what I mean?" Before Parker could respond, Virginia insisted, "Now, let her go. She wants down. She can't hurt anything. When my family visits they often bring a cat or a dog. Put her down. She wants to roam—sniff and snoop—snoop and sniff."

Parker lowered Olivia to the floor. The women chuckled when the sassy calico swished her tail twice, then trotted into the kitchen.

"What was that?" Virginia asked.

"Oh that tail," Parker said. "It's her way of communicating. She pets me with it, slaps me with it, and often gets the last word with it. That, I believe, was Olivia saying, 'It's about time you put me down. See ya later.'"

Virginia laughed out loud. "She is delightful. Just delightful."

"Can I help you?" Parker asked, following their hostess into the kitchen.

"Yes," Virginia said. "Thank you. I'll pour, and you can deliver."

Once the three of them were seated in the small, tastefully decorated living room with their tea, Virginia asked, "What brings you here, Mr. Caldwell? You said something about my old neighborhood." Suddenly she yelped, "Oopsie, off limits! Out of bounds! No kitties on the tea table."

"Oh, I'm so sorry," Parker said, quickly scooping Olivia from the beautifully arranged dining table. She released her to the floor and watched to see where she wanted to go.

"No harm done," Virginia said. "I do treasure that tea set, though. It's not your fault. Cats will be cats. We just have to help them learn their boundaries. Do you set boundaries for her in your home?"

Parker hesitated. "Um…well, I do try, but…"

"I know," Virginia said, laughing. "Like I said, cats are cats." She asked, "May I hold her? Can you bring her to me? Will she sit with me in my chair?"

"Certainly," Parker agreed, walking toward Olivia again.

"Wait," the woman said. "Let her finish sniffing, then she'll be ready to settle down." She leaned toward Olivia, who was now at her feet, and she put a hand on each side of the cat's face. "You sniff to your heart's content, beautiful, then come back here and we'll get to know each other." She motioned to Parker. "Just sit back down there. Let her go. She'll be just fine."

"Okay," Parker said hesitantly, not at all sure this was a good idea. She watched Olivia saunter away, her bushy tail waving from side to side.

Virginia also watched Olivia. She giggled. "I love her cute, fluffy derrière. Look at that swagger."

She laughed, then took a sip of tea and asked, "So Mr. Caldwell, what brings you here? Did you tell me that on the phone? If so, I've forgotten." She sat up straighter and lifted a finger in the air. "Oh, wait, it has something to do with my former neighbors, doesn't it?" She let out a sigh. "I sure miss some of my neighbors, but certainly not all of them. I was awfully glad when they turned that rundown old Gothic home into a dance studio or ballroom or whatever it is they do in there, but why they waited until I'd sold out, I don't know." She shuddered. "Those people living there were..." She looked at the others. "I dislike being narrow-minded or biased in any way when it comes to my fellow man, but I'm here to tell you there are some people that I have to wonder how they ever found their way here to this earthly plane and what their purpose is."

"To teach us to be more tolerant?" Parker suggested. She gazed into the hallway.

"Ophelia is fine," Virginia said. "Just fine. Don't you worry about her, now."

"Olivia," Parker corrected.

Virginia gazed at her and nodded. "Of course, Olivia." She chuckled. "I had a lifelong friend named Ophelia." She sighed. "I miss her."

In an attempt to regain Virginia's attention, Jud asked, "What people were you referring to, Mrs. Knudson?"

She tilted her head. "Excuse me?"

Jud explained, "You were talking about neighbors who you evidently had a problem with in your old neighborhood. Where did you live in that area, anyway?" he asked.

She chuckled. "It was an eclectic neighborhood, and it surely did change over the years. When it was developed early in the twentieth century, it was an area rich in fine architecture from that period. My home—the one my father built—is one of the last Victorian homes left," she frowned, "along with the Dunbars' hideous Gothic monstrosity."

Jud chuckled. "It doesn't sound like you approved of the style. It was a Victorian, though?" Jud asked. "Is Gothic a style of Victorian? It's from that period, right?"

"I guess it was considered a Victorian," Virginia said, "and no," she spat, "I did not like it." She backpedaled. "Well, I guess it was okay back in the day, but those people let it go to pot. I had to live there for all of those years watching that place deteriorate. If that wasn't bad enough, they moved in some teenagers who didn't have a clue about caring for a property like that, and they didn't give a rat's…" She looked sheepishly at Jud. "Well, it was a mess. I hated having to look at it out my sunroom window all the time. In fact, I finally pulled the drapes and kept them pulled." Virginia leaned toward Jud and spoke more quietly. "I didn't want to be in eyeshot of all that went on there. Did you ever see that horrid place?" Before Jud could respond, she continued, "Actually, I've been gone from the neighborhood now for nearly four years. It was after I left that they refurbished it. They bought additional property around there and built that hideous wall behind the place." She leaned forward and asked, "Now you tell me, what goes on in there? What are they hiding? No one seems to know, but you'd better believe there's a lot of speculation."

Jud shifted his position on the settee. Before he could comment, Virginia continued with a dramatic wave, "Truth be told, no one knew for sure what went on in that house even before it was reconstructed. It seemed to me that the Dunbars were as dark and mysterious as was that old Gothic Victorian of theirs." She took a deep breath, sat back, and closed her eyes. "That used to be an elite area known as Victorian Row. Well, not officially, but that's how most locals thought of that portion of Lake Drive. The houses and the grounds around the homes were splendid." She smiled and became more animated. "Can you imagine horse-drawn carriages waiting in front of those splendid homes, loading up with families dressed in their Sunday finery and on their way to church?" She looked at her guests. "That's the world I grew up in. Well, I was on the tail end of it. We still had a horse-drawn carriage, and Papa got it out occasionally, but by the time I knew what was what—you know, when I was six or seven years old—we were already riding around in automobiles."

Parker did a quick check to make sure Olivia was still curled up on a small ottoman. She smiled at the cat, then said, "It sounds like a lovely period to grow up in. I adore those ornate Victorian homes. So what happened? Did developers come in and demolish them to make room for tract homes?"

Virginia looked at Parker. "You haven't been to the area, have you? You haven't seen my home."

Parker shook her head. "We'll be visiting there this afternoon."

"Well, you can't miss my home—my former home. I just hope it doesn't fall victim to the popular notion of the rooming house or hippie pad—a place where young people convene. I've never seen a Victorian or even a stylish old Colonial survive that. In fact, that mentality caused the demise of nearly every other Victorian I know of in that area. Thankfully, I continued the care and upkeep of our home after my parents passed. I promised them I wouldn't let it fall into the hands of a slumlord or a developer, and I didn't," Virginia boasted.

"Tell us more about the Gothic Victorian," Parker suggested. "You know, the one you said was so rundown until they restored it—what—three years ago?" She glanced at Jud. "I think we heard that place was partitioned off into a two-family home at some point."

Virginia nodded. When she felt the cat push against her leg, she leaned forward and smiled. "Ophelia…um…I mean, Olivia, hello there. Want to come up here with me now? I'd love to sit and just pet your pretty fur. Come on, sweetie," she invited. She smiled when Olivia leaped up onto the arm of her chair. "I love this," she said, quietly petting Olivia." She giggled. "Look, she's caressing me with her tail. Now that's novel. I don't believe I've ever seen a cat do that—well, not to the degree your Olivia does with that magnificent tail of hers." She ran her fingers through Olivia's fur, then asked, "So where were we?"

Jud spoke first. "You were going to tell us about the Gothic house and the people who lived there."

"Yes," she said. "That's the Dunbar place. It was a hippie house for many years, and it didn't take long for the integrity of it—such as it was—to be lost. Those people ran it into the ground. Sure, the upkeep for those homes is expensive, but it's a shame to let them deteriorate like that. Sadly, over time I watched all of those majestic old homes go bad, one by one. First they'd become overrun with hippies. That was in the sixties and seventies. People would sell and the new owners, who had no ties to the beautiful old home and no concern for protecting the integrity of it, would open it to tenants—you know, rent out rooms. They weren't interested in doing any upkeep whatsoever, and their renters certainly didn't care. Rent was cheap, and they had a roof over their head. The old places were fragile, and with that sort of abuse, they began to fall apart. They deteriorated until they had to be condemned. They were eventually torn down and small single-family homes and duplexes took their place."

Virginia rested her head in her hand for a moment, saying, "It was so sad to see. So, so sad." She took a breath and sat up. "My home is the last one standing, at least the last one that maintains the integrity of its origin." She asked again, "Have you been out there? Have you seen my family home?" Without waiting for a response, she continued, "My daughter visited over the holidays, and she drove me out there to see it. I had sold it to a nice couple, and they moved in, all right, but they stay in only a small portion of the home and rent out the rest of it." She winced. "Like my daughter, Mo, said," she chuckled, "sorry, that's Maureen. My daughter's name is Maureen. She said that it could be so much worse."

"Worse?" Parker questioned. "What's going on there?"

"You haven't seen it?"

Parker shook her head. "Not yet."

Virginia smiled when Olivia snuggled down on her back in the chair next to her. "You are so cute," she crooned. She gently tickled the cat's tummy, then said, "Well, our former home isn't being used in its entirety as a family home, but it does look lovely. The new owners, the Bledsoes, are keeping it up, but like so many other people have done, they've succumbed to the trend of operating a touristy business from it. People love visiting shops in the old Victorians, or in forts, or former livery stables—you know. People crave shopping in or touring historical sites and buildings." She looked at Jud, then Parker. "Even the simplest of old buildings, as long as it has an interesting history or a unique design like the Victorians, will attract visitors. So the Beldsoes—Joe and Roberta, the people I sold to—are renting out space to a collection of creative people. There's a quilt shop; an art gallery; a framer—you know, picture framing; and I believe I saw someone making candles in the sunroom. I loved seeing the old homestead come back to life in such a unique and beautiful way, but it's still a shame that someone isn't enjoying the Victorian lifestyle that I knew growing up and even into my adulthood."

Parker smiled at the vision. She said quietly, "Sadly, those days are gone to us."

Virginia nodded.

"I'm sure you got some comfort from seeing your home still standing and in good repair," Jud said, "I mean when you visited the area with your daughter recently." He asked, "So you started to tell us about former neighbors that you had a problem with. Were they the people who lived in the—what did you call it—Gothic house?"

"Yes. Years ago they split that old relic into two homes. They called it a duplex, which I guess is technically correct, but it was actually a classic old Gothic partitioned off to accommodate two families. As I think I said, it's now some sort of exclusive business that attracts people from out of town."

"And you knew the people who lived there before all that happened?" Jud asked, attempting to keep Virginia focused.

"Yes!" she blurted. "Yes, they were terribly troublesome. They're the ones that caused me to rethink my tolerance level for human behavior. I'm certain there was something wrong with those people."

"Who lived there?" Parker asked.

Virginia watched Olivia jump down onto the floor. She gazed after her for a moment, then said, "Well, there were the young people on one side of it—the young men and a variety of young women coming and going." She spoke more quietly. "It's rumored that the matriarch—the grandmother of the boys—lived in the other side, but that was speculative."

"Why?" Parker asked. "I mean why was it speculative?"

"No one ever saw her, that's why," Virginia snapped. "Oh, there were lights on at various hours into the night, and the shades would go up and down with the dawn and the dusk, but there were no reliable reports of sightings. Even I, who lived nearby and who was home all the time, never ever saw a figure in the window on the south side of that house, nor did I see anyone go in or out of that portion of the old Gothic. Never!" she exclaimed.

Before the others could speak, Virginia raised her eyebrows. "Some say we did see her in local stores and on the streets and in church, but we didn't know it was her, because she was a master of disguise. Can you imagine? I found that theory hard to swallow, but what was the truth? No one knew."

Jud laughed. "It sounds like the Gothic house kept the rest of the neighborhood guessing."

"Oh yes," Virginia agreed. "That place was definitely the talk of the town, as they say." She grumbled, "It was downright mysterious and not in a pleasant way. If you ask me, there was way too much wasted energy put into the rumors and poured into the gossip that hinted at mysterious goings-on in that Gothic house, and we were all guilty of it, because those people were odd and a bit eerie." She sat back in her chair. "Except for one dear young woman. She loved cats too, but I must say I worried about her safety."

Before she could continue, they heard an odd sound coming from another room. The trio each looked at one another, then Parker stood up.

"Olivia!" She asked, "May I go see what she has done?"

"Yes," Virginia said, "by all means." She put her hands up to her face. "I hope it isn't Aunt Marie's vase. I probably should have put that in a closet or something." She winced. "I've had it repaired twice over the years when my own cats knocked it over."

"Oh, Olivia," Parker scolded upon gazing into the bedroom.

"Is it the vase?" Virginia called.

"No," Parker said, stepping into the hallway to report, "it's a bunch of papers and artwork. It looks like they were stacked on the chest at the foot of your bed."

"Yes," Virginia said. "I've been going through my art collection, and I heaped them up there until I could get back to the project. No problem." She frowned. "She didn't chew on the canvases or claw them, did she?"

Parker stepped closer to the clutter and called out, "It doesn't look like it. Okay if I pick these things up and stack them back on top of the chest?"

"Would you please?" Virginia asked. "Bring the cat in here and close the door." She giggled. "I'd like to cuddle some more. We were just getting to know each other." She placed her teacup on the saucer, scooted back in the chair, and prepared to take Olivia onto her lap.

Parker picked up the scattered papers and canvases, stacking them as neatly as possible on the chest. She started to pick up Olivia when the cat darted out into the hallway and disappeared. She glanced around the room to make sure nothing else had been disturbed, then she walked out, closed the door, and joined the others. She was surprised to find Olivia sitting in front of the detective, staring up at him.

Virginia leaned forward and pointed. "I think she brought you something, Mr. Caldwell. Do you see it there at your feet? She ran in here with it in her mouth and dropped it there."

Jud looked down at the cat. "What did you bring me, you silly pussycat?" He picked it up and examined it briefly. "It looks like one of your art pieces, Mrs. Knudson."

Everyone laughed when Olivia stood up and rested a paw on his knee. She reached out and pawed at the picture he held.

"Well, thank you," Jud said. "It was very nice of you to bring this to me, but I do believe it belongs to Mrs. Knudson. Can you take it to Mrs. Knudson?"

Parker walked closer to Olivia and ran her hand over her fur.

"Is she a cat burglar?" Virginia asked, chuckling.

"Not usually," Parker said, "but she's been hanging out with a klepto cat, lately, so maybe

Rags has taught her a few new tricks." She reached for the picture, but the detective pulled it back and looked at it more closely.

"Well, I'll be," he muttered. Somewhat abruptly he asked Virginia, "Where did you get this?"

Taken aback by his tone, Virginia said, "Um…well, let me take a look at it and maybe I can tell you. Why?"

"It's just that…" he started. He stood up and handed it to the woman.

"Oh yes," she said, smiling. "Lucy. She was one of the only delights coming from that awful Gothic bunch."

Parker chuckled and repeated, "Gothic bunch?"

Ignoring her, Virginia continued, "Lucy was a bright girl with enormous talent, but she seemed to have no drive, motivation, direction, or guidance." She shook her head in bewilderment. "Heaven knows I tried to motivate her, but those people seemed to have some sort of hold on Lucy. She didn't appear to have the capacity, the gumption, or the opportunity to shine, except in my eyes. Yes, Lucy is one of the very special things I miss about the neighborhood."

"Where is she?" Jud barked. "Do you know where she went after she left the Goth house? I guess that would have been when they did the renovation."

"Yes," she said. "It was after I moved in here that I heard what they'd done to the place. Neighbors were rejoicing to have those Gothic squatters gone."

"Squatters?" Parker questioned. "Weren't they part of the family who owned the house?"

"Yes," Virginia said, "but they never were accepted by the upstanding people of the community. So *squatters* describes them in my mind." She took a breath and spoke more tenderly. "As far as Lucy goes, I always hoped she'd break away from those people. I so wanted her to blossom, and it wasn't going to happen there."

"So the young people left the property?" Jud asked. "Do you know where they went? Do you know if Lucy went with them?"

Virginia shook her head. "I wish I did, but no. I never heard from her again. I was already living here, you see…"

"She didn't come here to visit you?" Jud asked.

"Heavens no," the woman said. "Lucy would never go this far away from that place alone. I'm sure of it." She chuckled. "In fact it was a cat that brought her to my doorstep—well, to my garden. I was outside picking a bouquet of spring flowers, you see, when one of Lucy's cats wandered over. She followed it and we became acquainted." She thought for a moment, then said, "No. In my view, Lucy lacked the ability to take that sort of step—you know, to find out where I was and make arrangements to visit me here. She'd walk the short distance to my home to visit me, but I can't see her taking a bus or hitching a ride to come out here. Sadly, all contact with Lucy has been lost. I don't know what happened to her. Why, Mr. Caldwell? Do you know that artist, Lucy?"

"I'm pretty sure I do," he said, his voice cracking. "I believe she's my daughter."

## Chapter Two

"Lucy?" Parker questioned as Jud drove away from the assisted-living home a while later.

He nodded. "Hannah Lucille. My wife insisted on naming her after a favorite aunt. This made her Aunt Lucille happy, but not Hannah. She hated her middle name, until she realized that Lucy could be a nickname. Then she began signing her drawings *Lucy*."

Parker picked up the picture. "Yeah, but there must be a lot of artists named Lucy. What makes you think your daughter did this? Is she an artist?"

"She enjoyed art growing up. Look at the style," he insisted. "She constantly drew cats as flowers, flowers as cats, cats with flower faces, cats among flowers, flowers with cat faces. That was her…you might say signature art. Speaking of her signature…" He pointed at the drawing in Parker's hands. "See how she signs it *Lucy* with a cat face in the U, and the Y becomes the cat's tail." He shook his head. "I don't know how she came up with that. It's pretty clever, don't you think so?"

"Yes," Parker said, "but Mrs. Knudson was unsure about identifying Hannah when you showed her that old photo of her you carry. Why do you think that was?"

"Like you said, it's an *old* photo. Hannah was maybe seventeen when it was taken and all dolled up for an event at school. Plus, a ninety-five year old probably doesn't have great eyesight. Yeah, she probably couldn't see it all that well. And it sounds like Hannah is or was letting her hair go." He shook his head. "My wife would not be happy to hear that. Hannah always took pride in her hair. She had nice hair and she took care of it. It's hard to imagine her with stringy, tangled hair." He glanced at the drawing that Parker still held in her hand. "If it wasn't for that evidence, I'd harbor a lot of doubt that the young woman Mrs. Knudson described is my daughter, but that drawing…" He couldn't finish.

"She seems to be very creative," Parker said, "…resourceful and creative, and," she looked down at the drawing again, "…fanciful."

Jud took a ragged breath and changed the subject. "That was really something when your cat brought that to me. And I sure appreciate Mrs. Knudson giving it to me." He winced. "I guess that's what people do once they reach their nineties. I remember my grandmother giving away things right and left. If someone admired something of hers, she'd give it to them." He laughed. "You had to be careful what you looked at in her house; you just might be carting it home whether you wanted it or not."

Parker ran her hand over Olivia's fur as the cat lay in her lap. "I think Olivia brought Mrs. Knudson a lot of pleasure today."

"Yeah, she did," Jud agreed. "I'm glad the cat climbed back up into the chair with her." He chuckled. "It sure sent that woman off on a jaunt down memory lane. She reminisced about every cat she'd ever known."

Parker nodded. "And she mentioned some of the cats your daughter had at the Goth house." She chuckled. "The stories Mrs. Knudson told about Lucy reminded me of myself with the barn cats. Oh, my folks let me have a few cats over the years that I could take into my bedroom, but for the most part I had to get my feline companionship with the barn cats." She faced him. "Why we had barn cats I don't know, because we didn't have barn animals—just a barn—but cats came, and I fed them and played with them. I guess I was the early version of a cat lady with my own colony of cats. Hmmm," she murmured, "I'll have to remember to put that on my next resume: 'colony cat lady at the age of eight.'"

Jud rolled his eyes. "Yeah, if you were applying for a job at a cat shelter, maybe. I doubt that would impress a magazine editor or a filmmaker." He slowed the car and changed the subject. "Here's that place. Yeah, it has what could be considered a Gothic look."

"It's Victorian Gothic," Parker said. "Or is it Gothic Victorian?"

"What does that mean, exactly?" he asked, watching Olivia climb into the backseat.

"I think it's probably a less extreme version of the Gothic architectural style, which can be terribly ornate and dark with a lot of pointy steeples." She chuckled. "Mrs. Knudson seemed to disapprove of it."

"Yeah, but it sounds like those people abused and neglected the place," Jud said. "No one who keeps up their property wants to see a rundown junker house in their neighborhood." He gazed through the car windows. "It's an impressive building now."

"It sure is," Parker said. "You'd never know it was once a shambles." She faced him. "So you believe this is where Hannah was living up until three years ago?"

He nodded, then muttered, "Dunbar."

"What?"

"Dunbar," he said. "That's the family's name. From what people have told us, it sounds like the Dunbar family still owns it. I wonder what kind of business they actually run in there."

"Virginia Knudson said it's a ballroom or a dance studio," Parker reminded him. She added,

"And isn't that what the gas station attendant told you?"

Jud nodded again. "But doesn't it seem like overkill? I mean it's so big. Well, he did say something about it being a spa, so maybe people get a spa treatment after they spend the day dancing."

"Do you think people can stay there? Is it a retreat for people who want to learn ballroom dancing?" she asked.

He nodded. "That could be, but why build such an intimidating wall around the backside of the property? What's the purpose of that? What do they keep inside that space?"

"I wonder if it's still home to some of the Dunbar clan." Parker suggested, "Maybe their housing is behind that wall." More quietly, she said, "Or they have something to hide."

"Like what?" he asked.

She shrugged. "Let's go find out."

Jud continued to stare out the car window, finally admitting, "I don't know if I could contain myself if I were to run into one of those Dunbar kids in there."

"Oh, so that's why you've been reluctant to check out this place?" she asked.

"You'd better believe it," he snarled. "Those damn kidnappers."

Parker faced him, asking, "You don't believe Hannah went with them of her own free will?"

"I don't know why she would," he spat, "or why she'd stay for all this time without contacting me." He winced. "But it appears from what Mrs. Knudson said that Hannah wasn't chained down or locked away. She had the freedom to come and go."

"Yes," Parker agreed, "but she didn't. According to Mrs. Knudson, Hannah walked over to her house, but really no place else, at least by herself."

"But why?" Jud asked, not expecting an answer. "Why did my bright, adventurous girl become submissive, maybe under the thumb of a bully? It's so out of character for her. What happened to change her so dramatically?"

Parker thought for a moment, then said quietly, "Maybe it was the shock of what happened on the mountainside that night. She might have lost friends in that mudslide, and look how close she came to being a victim. That sure could cause someone to break. She may also be suffering a serious case of survivor's guilt." Parker continued, "Who knows what she witnessed. I mean, according to that unfinished message she left on your wife's phone that night, she actually went back with those Dunbar boys to get her purse. She'd left her purse behind. That was after the slide. Remember, she said the road was covered with mud, and they couldn't get to the campsite where she'd left her purse." She spoke more quietly. "What did she see or hear on the hillside that night?"

46

Jud stared straight ahead, and Parker continued, "Hannah came frighteningly close to dying that night, and something like that can certainly mess with your mind. At the very least, she could have fallen into a debilitating depression."

"I guess that's possible," he said. "She was already upset about her mother's illness, so maybe that *is* what happened." He shook his head. "But she just didn't seem to be the kind of girl who would break that easily or who'd follow someone who would take her away from her family." He hit the steering wheel a couple of times and snarled, "Not knowing sucks."

"You know that she's probably alive," Parker said quietly. "At least as recently as four years ago she was alive."

"Yeah, if that girl Mrs. Knudson befriended was actually Hannah," Jud muttered.

"What are you doing?" Parker asked as the detective pulled away from the curb. "Aren't we going in? I want to see what's inside that place— you know, what goes on in there." She turned in her seat. "I mean, look at the caliber of clientele they get. Almost all the cars out front are mega-buck cars. Why aren't we going in?" she whined.

"Not yet," he said. "I want more information." He faced her briefly as he drove.

"Didn't you learn that in school or wherever you studied investigative writing?"

"Learn what?" she asked.

"To take it slow and easy until you have enough information to call someone out or detain them," he explained.

"So where are we going now?" she asked.

"Remember, I told you we have an appointment with that realtor."

"Oh yes, Mr. Atkinson," Parker said. She peered into the backseat and smiled at Olivia, who lay sound asleep on her blanket. "Nice office," she said minutes later as Jud slowed the car and parked in front of a modern building in what seemed to be the hub of the village. "He's a realtor?" she asked.

"And property manager," Jud said. "From the looks of it he's pretty busy. Have you noticed all the *for-sale* signs and how many of them have *sold* signs attached? It looks like real estate is booming here."

Parker nodded. "From what we've seen, this area is in need of some upgrades—maybe not as elaborate as what they did to the Dunbar place, though." She got out of the car and reached for Olivia through the back passenger door. "Come on, sleepy girl," she crooned.

"She's going in there with us?" Jud questioned.

"I told you, I don't leave her in the car." Parker kissed Olivia's cheek. "I did once and it didn't go well. I'd stupidly left her to guard a cake I was taking to a friend's house while I picked up a few last-minute things at a minimart. Not only did she do damage while I was gone for those scant few minutes, but she put me on a guilt trip you wouldn't believe." She snuggled with Olivia. "Seeing that sweet face against the car window when I returned and hearing the pitiful meows…I felt so awful." Sternly, she said, "Then I saw what she'd done to the cake. I'd spent an hour decorating that thing and I returned to the car to find…well, it wasn't a pretty sight."

Jud chuckled. "So you had to toss the cake and buy minimart donuts for the party?" He laughed heartily. "Was she all covered in frosting?"

"No," Parker insisted. "The cake was for my friend's child's birthday. Olivia didn't actually touch it. It was tucked into a box, but she must have stepped on the top of the box, rolled across it, ran across it…The frosting was all woopsie-doodle-crazy, but the cake was edible. I was ribbed relentlessly by my friends, but the kids loved it and they had a ball playing with Olivia."

"She likes kids?" Jud asked.

Parker smiled. "She loves kids and old people."

Once inside the building, Jud motioned. "There's suite three." When they entered, he approached the receptionist and announced, "Judson Caldwell. We have an appointment with…"

"Oh yes," the woman said enthusiastically, "he's expecting you. Please, go on in." She did a double-take and asked Parker, "Is that a cat?"

Parker smiled. "Yes, this is Olivia."

The receptionist stood up. "Oh no, ma'am, Mr. Atkinson has allergies. I don't think you'd better go in there with the cat or even with cat fur on your clothing. I'm sorry, but I'll have to ask you to leave with the cat."

Jud grinned at Parker. "Better go put her in the car."

"I'll wait outside," Parker said. "You go in."

"But…" he started.

"Go on. You know what to ask. I'll be outside walking Olivia."

"So, how did it go?" Parker asked when Jud caught up to her and Olivia fifteen minutes later.

He chuckled. "I knew we should have left the cat in the car. I could have used your help in there. We don't have any cake in the car; she would have been just fine."

Parker shook her head and emphasized, "I *don't* leave her in the car. It's dangerous for many reasons. No. Don't even go there."

"Well, what good is she when she's banned from our interviews?" he complained.

Parker grinned. "You might be surprised."

"Huh?"

"Sit," Parker invited, scooting over on the low block wall to make room for Jud while she watched Olivia roam at the end of her leash. "So what did you learn?" she asked.

"That the Dunbar crowd wasn't exactly popular in the neighborhood."

"Well, you knew that already," she reminded him. "Mrs. Knudson sure wasn't a fan."

He nodded and continued, "Yeah, and some homeowners even sold out because of the Dunbar kids. I guess there'd been complaints about them over the years, but nothing serious enough to evict them or anything. Oh!" he chirped, "I found out where the money came from."

"The Dunbar family money? You did?" Parker asked. "Where? I mean, it seems like such a stretch from a rundown, falling-apart house to what we saw this morning—that over-the-top whatever-you'd-call-it. It's new and all, but you have to admit it's an oddball structure compared to the flavor of this town." She tilted her head. "So where did the money come from?"

He cleared his throat. "Well, I guess it was old family money. They'd been sitting on it for years. No one knows why or even where it came from in the first place—you know, how the original Dunbars made their money."

Thinking out loud, Parker said, "It would sure be interesting to find out. That would be an important piece for my article." When Jud narrowed his eyes at her, she added, "Once we have a happy ending, of course." She thought for a moment and said, "So the Dunbars have a family secret. I wonder if they had mafia ties."

Ignoring her comment, Jud glanced at Olivia and asked, "So what did you mean when you said I'd be surprised about something the cat did? What happened? Did something happen?"

"It sure did," Parker said. "I was sitting here watching Olivia scout for bugs and forage around when this woman walked up with a cute little wiggly-butt dog that wanted nothing more than to play with Olivia. His name is Baxter, and he was so excited to meet her. Olivia, on the other hand, wasn't so sure about him."

"Does she even like dogs?" Jud asked.

"Actually yes," Parker said, "especially calm, quiet dogs. It doesn't matter how big or small they are, as long as the dog is calm and quiet." She chuckled. "Well, so she sees this little dog, and she's mildly interested in getting to know him, but he's bouncing all over the place and making her nervous, so she slaps him a good one."

"With her claws?" he asked, amused.

Parker nodded. "Poor little thing. He let out a good yelp and withdrew. He sat down, tilted his cute little head from side to side, and looked at Olivia like she'd hurt his feelings big time. It was pitiful, but it caused Baxter to calm down, and that gave Olivia a chance to communicate with him on *her* terms." Parker giggled. "About the only way you can get along with a cat is on the cat's terms, you know."

"I'll remember that," Jud said. He pushed against his knees and started to stand up. "Are you ready to go?"

"There's more," she said, grinning.

"What?" he complained, sitting back down on the wall. "Parker, I have better things to do today than listen to your cat-and-dog stories."

"I think you'll want to hear this one," she said. "Baxter's owner, Theresa, used to clean for the Dunbar family."

"Oh?" he asked, perking up. "When? What time period?"

"I guess as recently as five years ago," Parker said.

He faced her and asked more quietly, "How did you get onto that topic with a stranger? We don't want to spread word too far and wide about our interest in the Dunbar family. I'd like to keep our activity and intent under wraps as much as possible."

Parker challenged, "Really? And how do you expect to do that when you've already talked to some of the very people who are most likely to broadcast our mission and intent."

"Who?" he asked.

"A long-standing citizen who knows everyone in town and probably everyone's business…"

"Virginia?" he asked.

She nodded. "And a realtor. Realtors get around. They talk to people, and they attend meetings. They know all, and they probably tell all. Have you ever known a realtor who didn't know everyone's secrets?"

"Okay, okay," Jud said, "so we're not being all that discreet. Still, we want to be talking to the right people, not just anyone who walks past with a cute dog." He stared down at Olivia, who wound herself around his ankles sniffing his shoes. He asked, "So what did she tell you? It had better be good."

"I think so," Parker said. She handed him the cat's leash so he could untangle it from around his legs. "Theresa said it was like a revolving door of girls at that place—you know, the Dunbar house—before it was remodeled, but she said that only a few stayed. It seemed to Theresa that it was a particular type of girl who stayed—smart, well-mannered, and relatively self-sufficient, which seemed odd to me. I mean, we don't know what was going on in that house or what goes on in there today, but I would have guessed they were *kept* women. I imagined them to be weak, needy followers, unless…"

"Unless?" Jud repeated.

"Well, unless there's a payoff for them—the girls are getting something from the situation."

"Such as?" Jud asked with a confrontational tone. "Are you suggesting it's a sex ring? Are you referring to that kind of kept woman?"

Parker gasped. "I hope not. No. I don't know what it might be—just a place where young women go because they feel they belong, maybe—where they can flop for next to nothing and smoke or drink or do drugs or just be lazy, and where no one will nag them. So, yeah, I imagined a totally different type of girl than Hannah falling into that lifestyle— at least from the way you describe her."

He thought for a moment, took a deep breath, and asked, "Did you ask her about Hannah?"

"Do you mean Lucy?" she asked. "It sounds like she's known as Lucy around here—if, in fact she's actually Hannah." She stood up and walked the leash around a plant behind the wall to give Olivia more slack.

"Yes, if, in fact," Jud repeated, quietly.

Parker stood a distance away, allowing Olivia a wider range in which to explore. She said, "Theresa mentioned Lucy by name, saying she's one of those who stayed. She even spoke to her once about her role there, and she was sorry she did, because she believes that's why she lost her job."

"The house cleaner lost her job because she spoke to Hannah?" Jud questioned.

Parker nodded. "That afternoon as she was preparing to leave after her work day, one of the Dunbar boys handed her an envelope and said they would no longer need her services."

"Are you saying he didn't like someone questioning one of his harem?" Jud asked, choking up.

Parker moved closer to him and said, "Jud, I don't think that's it. Theresa indicated that the termination notice did not come from one of the young people. There was someone else making the decisions in that household—someone she never met."

"What?" he asked, frowning.

"Well, I could be wrong, but I got that the young men were not in charge, and that whoever was did not want their identity known. Lucy may have revealed a secret that day or enough of a secret that it made that person nervous, and that's the reason Theresa was let go." When Jud didn't respond, Parker added, "You might be putting the blame for Hannah's disappearance on the wrong person. The Dunbar boys might just be puppets."

Jud allowed Parker's words to digest, then he asked, "So did she tell you where this girl went after they did the remodel? Does the housekeeper know what happened to her?"

Parker shook her head. "I'm afraid not."

"There isn't much known about that bunch, is there?" he muttered. He slapped his knee and stood up. "Well, let's get a move on. I want to check out the neighborhood more thoroughly—you know, talk to a few more people and get a clearer picture of the situation. That's how you make real progress in your investigation. You have to know something in order to learn something. Otherwise, especially when your emotions are involved, you come across sounding like a lunatic and no one will tell you anything."

Parker grinned as she stepped into the car with Olivia. "We wouldn't want that to happen."

He nodded, then glanced at her briefly while starting the car. "Yeah, and I expect you to keep me focused and levelheaded."

"Now, that's a tall order." When she realized Jud probably wasn't in the mood for snide remarks, she asked, "So what's the plan?"

"I think we should knock on doors. I want to find someone who's familiar with that crowd from the Goth house—someone they socialized with, who actually knows them and who knows where they went."

"But you do want to visit that building, don't you—the old homestead?" Parker asked. "You want to see if Hannah left a mark or a clue or something inside there, right?"

He winced. "That seemed like a good idea when you first mentioned it, but after seeing the place, I doubt there's much left of the original. I think we can toss that idea out the window. We may have to look elsewhere for a tangible clue from Hannah."

"Tangible?" Parker repeated.

"Even subtle—I don't care. Something," he stressed, "just something."

"Like that drawing Olivia brought to you?" Parker suggested.

He nodded. "Yes. You see, that's a clue telling us that she most likely *was* here. Hannah was here alive, and…" Thinking out loud, he continued, "Maybe not well, but she was here and alive. I think she needs help. We have to find her before it's too late." He took a deep breath and pulled up to a curb near the Dunbar building.

Parker pointed. "Look, I'll bet that's Virginia Knudson's home out there in the distance. Isn't it grand? I want to get closer and see the detail in the architecture, don't you?" She glanced back at what had been the Dunbar house. "It really is different from that place—they're both Victorians, but so different. The Dunbar place is dark."

"That's what Gothic is—dark, foreboding, sinister..." he explained.

"Very good," she complimented.

"What?" he asked.

"Good definition of Gothic. You sound like a walking thesaurus." She asked, "Can we visit Virginia's old house? I want to see the inside. It's open to the public, you know."

"First things first," Jud groused, unbuckling his seat belt.

Parker stepped out of the car with Olivia in her arms and glanced at the former Knudson home again. "It's sure more inviting than that dark house."

Jud motioned with his head. "Come on, let's knock on some doors."

"I'd better let Olivia have a moment," Parker said, placing her on the ground and holding tightly to her leash.

"Have a moment?" he complained. "Is she going to meditate, fix her makeup? What does she need a moment for?"

Parker tilted her head and said more quietly, "A potty break. Ever hear of a potty break? Cats need them too."

"Oh, so a spa day," he quipped. "Why didn't she go in the flower bed back at the real estate office?"

"How uncouth," Parker remarked.

Jud asked, "Do you have one of those poop bags—you know, that people carry when they're walking their dogs?"

She chuckled. "No. She's a cat. She flushes when she's finished."

"What do you mean, she flushes?" he criticized.

"She buries it, okay?" Parker hissed, following Olivia around an area of dirt on an empty lot.

"Well?" Jud said. "When's she going to—you know?"

"When she's good and ready," Parker spat. To Olivia she said, "Can you get on with it, girl? You're making the detective uncomfortable." She then said, "Ahhh. You found the right spot. Good girl." She chuckled when she saw Jud standing a distance away, facing in the opposite direction with his arms crossed.

"Is she finished?" he asked impatiently.

"Almost," Parker said. "After she does a little personal grooming.

"You've gotta be kidding me, Parker," he complained.

"Okay, okay," she said, picking up Olivia and trotting up to him.

"Geez Louise, cat," he groaned, leading the way along a cracked cement walkway toward a small house badly in need of paint.

"Why here?" Parker asked quietly. "This is probably the most run-down place on the block."

Jud removed a picture from his pocket. "Virginia Knudson gave me this while you were, um, taking a personal break back at the old-folks home. It's a picture of the Dunbar place five, six, or maybe ten years ago."

"Ewww," Parker said, wrinkling her nose. "It was a mess." She looked back at the remodeled home. "What a difference. It's still dark, but at least it's well-maintained and kind of interesting with all those steeply pitched roofs." She looked at the photo again and frowned. "It sure had a sinister look to it before the remodel."

"Yes," Jud said, "and the Dunbar kids lived there when it was a pigsty. What sort of conditions do you imagine their closest friends would live in?"

"Oh, I get it," Parker said. "You figure that their friends probably live in squalor like they did."

"Squalor?" he repeated. "That's probably overkill. I mean, my daughter wouldn't live in squalor, but yeah, you're getting the idea."

Parker nodded. "Okay, let's check out some of these people."

"Thanks for your approval," he said snarkily, continuing along the path to the house.

Parker grimaced. Her voice pinched, she said, "I hope they don't invite us in."

The pair knocked on the doors of four houses before someone finally answered. "Where is everyone today?" Jud mused, annoyed.

"What are you, a door-to-door salesman?" the woman responded curtly. "No one around here answers to solicitors. They don't open the door to servers, either. Are you a server?"

"Server?" Parker repeated.

"Summons server," the woman clarified. "Which are you, a solicitor or a summons server?"

"None of the above," the detective said. "We're looking for someone."

"Oh," the woman yelped. "Well, that's another level of concern for some of the people around here." She eyed the couple and asked, "Are you cops?"

"No," Jud said. "I'm Judson Caldwell and this is Parker Campbell…"

When the woman saw the calico cat in Parker's arms she brightened. "And who is this gorgeous creature?"

Parker smiled. "This is Olivia."

"My, my," the woman said. "Such an aristocratic name for such a pretty cat." She chuckled. "Around here cats are Smokey, Fluff, and Miss Kitty. Oh there's a cat called Stinky that hangs out around the corner." She squinted at Olivia. "Is she lost? Are you trying to find her owner?" She reached her arms out. "Heck, I'll take her." She looked at Parker suspiciously. "She's housebroke isn't she?"

Parker grinned. "Yes, but she's not lost. She's *my* cat. We're here to get information about a missing person."

"Maybe you know her or knew her before she moved away three years ago," Jud said. "Have you lived here for long?"

"Two years," the woman said.

Jud slumped, and the woman pointed. "I lived in the yellow house back there before that, and across the street before that. I work at the café up the road a ways and have for darn near twenty years. Yeah, I've been around this neighborhood for most of my life. Why?"

Jud made brief eye contact with Parker, then said, "May we come in and talk to you for a few minutes, Mrs…"

"Ms," she corrected, "Lydia Strickland." She thought for a moment, smiled at Olivia, and said, "Yeah, sure. Come in, but I'll have to leave soon. I have some errands to run before my shift." She motioned toward a small sitting room that opened up into a dinette and kitchen. "Please, won't you sit down?"

"Ms. Strickland," Jud started.

"Lydia," she insisted. "Call me Lydia; everyone around here does."

"Okay, Lydia," Jud said, sinking into an overstuffed chair in need of reupholstering. "How well did you know the people who lived in the old house up the street there—the one that's now a dance studio or whatever?"

"The Dunbar place? Which people?" she asked.

"I assume they would have been the most recent tenants before it was refurbished. Did you know anyone there named Brad or Travis?"

Lydia frowned. "Not well. I'm not a part of their inner circle or anything. That family has actually been here longer than I have, but I never had much occasion to know them outside of the café." She leaned forward. "They were a strange bunch, and they kept to themselves a lot. Brad kind of scared me when he was growing up and his cousin, Travis, too. Yeah, they were odd, but that's what you can expect from a family tree like theirs." She smiled. "Some of the young ladies in the house seemed nice, enough."

This piqued Jud's interest. He blurted. "Did you know the young women? I'm interested in one in particular, the one known as Lucy. She's an artist. At least she was dabbling in art while she lived in this area."

"Sure," Lydia said. "Lucy was a favorite of everyone at the café. She had manners, that one, but I sure didn't like…" She stopped and looked at Jud. "Why? Why do you want to know about Lucy? Is she the missing person you mentioned? Is she a runaway?"

Jud thought about the question, and said, "Possibly more like a kidnap victim. Lydia, did you get the impression that she was being held against her will?"

"No," she said. "All those girls seemed to be free to come and go." She shrugged and added, "Only they didn't, as I recall. Yeah, that was odd. The gals I work with would sometimes comment about Lucy's demeanor. One of them actually discussed Lucy with a cop who comes into the café."

"Why?" Jud asked eagerly. "Did they suspect she was being held hostage?"

Lydia stared across the room at him and shook her head. "No, not really. It was because she just seemed a little off from the normal, and we were afraid someone might be taking advantage of her." She asked, "Do you know Lucy? Is she slow?"

"No!" Jud blurted. "I mean I might know her, but the Lucy I know—no, she is not slow in the way I think you mean. Say, do you have a picture of her? Did anyone ever take a picture of the girl named Lucy?"

Lydia thought for a moment, then muttered, "I might have saved that newspaper photo. Let me take a look." She started to leave the room, then asked, "Can I get you something to drink?"

Both Jud and Parker declined.

"Where do you think *you're* going?" Parker asked, allowing Olivia to jump down to the floor, but still holding tightly to the leash.

"Dive in anytime, Parker," Jud said quietly once Lydia had disappeared into another room. "You know, if you have any pertinent questions."

She nodded.

"Well, I found it," Lydia said, returning. "It doesn't often happen that I can put my fingers on something at the exact moment I want it." Her smile brightened. "Well, what do we have here? Miss Olivia, you're in my chair. Do you want to sit with me?"

"I'm sorry," Parker said, standing up. "I'll get her."

"No. Please, let her stay. I'd love to spend some time in her kitty-cat energy. That would be a great boost to my day." She handed Jud the newspaper clipping. "That's Lucy and that bunch at the Independence Day parade maybe five years ago. I saved it because the little boy on the bicycle in front of them is my nephew. He's thirteen now." Lydia sat down with Olivia and asked, "Is she the Lucy you're looking for?"

Jud nodded. "Yes. I see what you mean about her demeanor. She looks drugged or something."

"Yeah," Lydia said, "or something." She leaned forward and spoke more quietly. "Some here in town think it's a spell."

"A spell?" Parker asked. "What sort of a spell? From where?"

"It's more like from whom?" Lydia said. She glanced at the others, carefully lowered Olivia to the floor, and stood up. "I'd better get myself ready to go. I guess you got what you came for, right? I answered your questions."

"Yes you did," Jud said, "but I have one more question that I sure hope you or someone around here can answer. "Where is…Lucy now?"

"And I have a question," Parker said. "Are you suggesting that Lucy has been caught up in a cult or something—black magic, witchcraft—that kind of spell?"

Lydia glanced at her, then at Jud, and shook her head. "I think that's all I can give you. As far as I know, Lucy hasn't been seen around here since they started renovating the Dunbar place." She smiled. "It's really rather beautiful, isn't it—I mean in a medieval sort of way? It sure doesn't harmonize with the rest of the neighborhood." She rolled her eyes and added, "But then, it never did." She chuckled, then asked, "Have you been inside?"

Parker shook her head. "No, we haven't. Have you? Do you know what goes on in there?"

"Dance, I'm told, but no. No one from around here has been inside. The clientele are all from out of town. We're thinking it's some sort of highfalutin resort for the rich with maybe secret and private amenities."

"What?" Jud questioned. "Are you suggesting it's a brothel?"

Lydia laughed. "No. I don't think so. Some neighbors are suspicious in that way, but no, I think it's more esoteric—not something anyone from around here would even understand or be interested in. Know what I mean?" Before Jud could speak, Lydia walked toward the door and opened it. "It's been nice talking to you. Thanks for coming by. I'm sorry I couldn't help more, but I do have some advice. I offer this for your health and well-being. Go home. Let Lucy be. She has made a choice. I believe that. Go home," she said, closing the door behind them.

Jud and Parker stood outside on Lydia's porch for a moment before walking away with Olivia.

"That didn't go very well," Jud mumbled, walking slowly with Parker toward his car.

"I'd say it was telling," Parker said. "Very telling, only…"

"What do you mean?" he insisted.

"Well, now we know that Hannah was here. We have the family name of the men she's with—or was with. We have a little background on the family and the…ahem…mystery house, and we know where it is." Just then she edged her phone from her pocket. After looking at the screen for a few moments, she said, "Listen, Jud, Houston is on his way to my place. Would you mind taking me back to my car?"

"Oh, your boyfriend?" he grumbled, opening the car door for her.

"Yes. I told you he was coming, and I really want to see him before he heads back to Texas."

"So he follows the rodeo circuit, does he?" Jud asked. Quietly, he said, "That was an aspiration of my daughter's at one time."

"Really? Does she ride?" Parker asked.

"I don't know what in the hell she does now," he complained, "but yeah, the wife put her in lessons, and she did some shows. She seemed to enjoy that, but then…"

"What happened?" Parker asked quietly.

"Well, I suppose what happens in many homes across America. Kid wants pony. Parents can't afford to feed one, so they appease the kid as much as possible with lessons on someone else's pony. Kid loses interest either because she's a kid or because you can't give her the whole enchilada with her own horse and a place to keep it."

"You have a great place for a horse," Parker reminded him.

"Yeah, but it was too little, too late. Hannah had already started to lose interest in horses, and I blame myself for that. I'm the one who dragged my feet when it came to…"

The couple rode without speaking for a few minutes, then Parker asked, "What will you do for the next few days?"

"Probably poke around a bit from a distance until you get back," he said.

She faced him. "Jud, you're an experienced investigator. What do you need me for?"

"Are you ready to quit me?" he challenged.

"No," she said. "Not at all. It's just that… well, you seem to be relying on me a lot."

He sighed deeply. "I just don't want to make a mistake. Parker, I'm too close to this thing. I don't trust the department to take over, not with what we may be dealing with." He glanced at her as he drove. "I'm getting the impression that we could be tapping into something bigger than we know, and I don't want my daughter in any danger." He shook his head. "I don't trust myself because I'm too emotionally—well, this is emotional for me. I expect you to keep me from doing something stupid."

"Whoa. No pressure there," she quipped. She thought for a moment and said, "Okay, I get it."

"Do you have something else you'd rather or should be doing?" he asked.

Parker grinned. "Well, for the next few days, yes. I want to be with Houston. But beyond that, as long as I have time to do the writing I've promised to do for my agent, no, there's nothing I'd rather be doing than helping you find your daughter and being a part of bringing her home."

"Well, good then. You go enjoy your time with your guy, and I'll do more research and maybe linger in the background in this community."

She studied him for a moment. "Why don't you do something just for you? Get out and play."

"Play?" he repeated.

"Is that a foreign concept for you? Didn't you ever learn to play?" she asked. "You know, shoot pool, toss horseshoes, just sit in your shop with a buddy or a couple of neighbor guys and talk about old times or fixing cars or something." More lightly she said, "You like to go to swap meets and yard sales. Have you done that lately?"

He shook his head. "No. Most recently I've been hanging out where the wild cats are—you know, at the disaster site. But now that the department has taken that over, and I know my daughter isn't among the victims, I stay away. As you know, I have a new focus or a new direction when it comes to finding her." He drove into the parking lot at the restaurant where they'd had breakfast earlier, pulled up next to Parker's SUV, and nodded. "Here we are. There's your car. Go have fun with Houston."

"Okay," she said, opening the car door. She stared at him for a moment, then said, "When we find Hannah, you and I are going to do something fun. Hey, Hannah may want to join us."

"What do you mean?" he asked suspiciously. "I'm not going to ride a horse or anything like that."

"Then we'll take a hike or go out on Jet Skis or fly a kite at the beach or go up in a hot air balloon. We'll do whatever you want to do as long as it's something that will make us laugh and maybe even giggle."

He chuckled. "Giggle, huh? We'll see about that." He motioned with his head. "Now go. Have fun. I'll be fine. Hey," he added.

"What?" she asked.

"Thanks." He reached out and ruffled Olivia's fur. "Be good pussycat."

Parker smiled at the detective as she climbed out of his car.

Parker had been home just long enough to finish editing her latest story. She pushed *send* and let out a sigh. *Now to flesh out the story about the missing persons being found after seven years. To think that those innocent people have been buried all that time under a thick blanket of mud less than five miles from where most of them lived.* She shook her head, thinking, *Those families finally have closure—or will once the DNA results are official.* She gazed across the room at Olivia, who sat on the bed preening. "That was one bittersweet case, wasn't it, love-love?" She smiled at the cat. "You've sure settled in here. We've been in this condo for, what—less than two weeks, and you're so relaxed, like you've lived here all your life." She chuckled. "We've never stayed anywhere for long since we've been together. We're vagabonds, that's what we are."

Suddenly Olivia stopped licking and stared curiously into the hall. Parker chuckled. "How you get into those crazy yoga positions is a mystery to me. Look at you," she said, "you have one paw behind your head, and I can't even see where the other one is… Oh, Olivia, you must have elastic in your spine." When Olivia leaped off the bed and trotted out of the room, Parker said, "I think you're right, someone's at the door." She followed the cat into the living room. "Is your favorite man here?" she asked, giddily. "Yes, that's probably him." She opened the door widely, but her welcoming smile faded when she saw who stood in the doorway. "Pamela. My goodness, what…? I mean how? Gee, kiddo, I didn't expect you. Would you like to come in?"

Pamela smiled. "I sure would. That's why I drove all the way up here."

Parker picked up Olivia to make sure she didn't dart out the door, and she ushered Pamela inside.

"I can tell you're surprised to see me," Pamela said, "but maybe not happily surprised, right cousin?" She cringed as she placed her purse and jacket on an empty chair. "I guess I should have called ahead, but—well, frankly, I was afraid you would turn me away."

"How…" Parker started.

"How did I get your address?" Pamela explained, "I saw where your mother had written it." She glanced around. "Were you in the middle of something?"

"Kind of, yes," Parker said, still stunned by the woman's presence. "Um…sit down and tell me what's going on." Parker started to take a seat, then offered, "Can I get you a bottle of water, or…"

"Do you have coffee?" Pamela asked. "I know it's late in the day, but I do love my coffee, and I didn't see a coffee shop on my way here."

"Sure. I can make some," Parker agreed.

"I'll help," Pamela offered, following her toward the kitchen. She stopped. "Okay if I use your…um facility? I've been driving straight for, like, three hours."

"Sure." Parker nodded to her right. "It's at the end of the hall."

"Nice place," Pamela said when she returned. "How long are you staying here? Your mom said this is just temporary. She says you have a place out near Palm Springs someplace, but you're rarely there."

Parker nodded. "Yeah, I'm not sure how long I'll be here. I've rented it for another few weeks, but I can extend that if I give the landlady enough notice. If I leave early, there might be a penalty."

Pamela gazed around the room. "Yeah, I could live like this."

"Pamela," Parker said, facing her, "is Mom okay? You two haven't had a falling out or…"

"Not really," Pamela said. "We get along pretty well, actually. I just have these yearnings sometimes to fly away—you know, to try something different and experience a new place."

"What about your job?" Parker asked.

Pamela waved dismissively. "Oh, that wasn't much of a job. For me, jobs are a dime a dozen. I've never been attached to one—you know, that held my interest for long."

"Well, Pamela, maybe if you'd follow your passion…"

"What passion?" she asked. "A job is a job. Who has a passion for working?"

Parker studied her cousin for a moment, then said, "Well, I do. I know a lot of people who do. Work is an important part of our lives. We need it to survive financially, and we really should choose work that fulfills something within ourselves or that makes us feel good about the contribution we're making. Don't you think so?"

"I never thought about work like that," Pamela said. She shrugged. "I guess I never had a job that meant anything to me." She chuckled. "Don't you know there are other ways to survive? I've found several—men, the system," she grinned and added, "family." She tilted her head and looked toward the living room. "Was that a knock at the door? Are you expecting someone?"

Parker nodded, placed a cup of coffee on the bar counter in front of Pamela, and dashed into the living room.

Pamela watched as Parker opened the door to a tall, good-looking man dressed in jeans and a Western shirt, complemented by an oversized belt buckle. When she saw the man grab Parker and swing her around before lowering her to the floor and kissing her passionately, she said to Olivia, who sat on a barstool next to her, "I guess she *was* expecting someone. Wow! Do you know who that is?"

Olivia stood up and swished her tail from side to side as if annoyed, then she sat back down alongside Pamela and continued watching the display in the living room.

"Pamela," Parker said moments later, walking into the kitchen with her guest, "this is Houston. You probably heard us talking about him at Christmas. Houston, this is my newly found cousin, Pamela."

"Newly found?" he asked, looking from one of them to the other.

"Yes," Parker said more brightly. "Pamela joined us at Mom's for Christmas last month. Her mother was Mom's sister." Parker winced. "My aunt died after Pamela was born, and Mom and Dad raised Pamela until her father came and took her and kept her hidden from us for many years." She smiled at Pamela and added, "She just recently found her way back home."

"Oh!" Houston said, stunned. He reached out a hand. "Hello, Pamela. Nice to meet you. Welcome."

Pamela smiled widely and shook Houston's hand.

"Can I get you a cup of coffee or a beer or something?" Parker asked.

"Well, I'll take a beer," Pamela said. "I didn't know beer was an option."

Parker faced her cousin. "Pamela, I don't think that's a good idea, and I'll tell you why."

"I'm all ears," Pamela quipped. She grinned and added, "I am of age, you know."

Ignoring her attempt at humor, Parker said, "Listen, Houston is here for only two days before he heads to Texas. We haven't seen each other since just before Christmas."

"Oh!" Pamela said. "I get it."

"So you'll be driving yourself to a motel, and I'm not going to send you off with alcohol in your system," Parker explained.

"Hey, you have two bedrooms here. I saw two bedrooms, so no problem. I'll be as quiet as a mouse. You won't even know I'm here. I just need a place to crash until I decide what to do next." Pamela admitted sheepishly, "I didn't get my last check, so I don't have any money."

"What was wrong with Mom's place?" Parker asked.

"Nothing. It's nice. Your mom's great. Like I said, I just got bored. I get bored easily." Pamela grinned. "Your mom said I take after you, so I figured you'd understand."

Parker put her hands on her hips. "Pamela, you can't stay here, that's all there is to it. Aren't there homeless shelters where you can crash until you know which direction you want to go—what you want to do next? I'll take you to lunch or dinner or something after Houston leaves."

"Sure, there are shelters," Pamela said, "but they aren't as nice as this is. Besides, I like my privacy."

Houston saw Olivia looking at him from the countertop, and he picked her up and cradled her. "Hi, pretty girl," he crooned. "Have you been behaving yourself?" When he realized that the women weren't getting very far in their negotiations, he suggested, "Babe, why don't you let your cousin stay here with the cat and we can—you know—get a room someplace?"

"No," Parker said emphatically. "I want us to stay here. I have plans." She looked at Pamela. "Plus, my cousin isn't very familiar with pets. I think Olivia might be more than she can handle."

"Parker," he complained, "she's a cat. What could be so hard about taking care of a cat—feed her, clean up her poop, let her sleep. All cats want to do anyway is sleep."

Parker grinned at him and shook her head. "You haven't spent enough time with this cat, buddy. She requires practically twenty-four-hour surveillance to keep her out of trouble." When he didn't seem convinced, she added, "You should have seen the disturbance she created at the Malibu police station when she was arrested on Christmas Eve."

"What?" Houston exclaimed.

Parker waved a hand in the air. "I'll tell you about it later." She faced Pamela. "So like I said, Houston and I have plans, and we weren't planning on a third wheel. You and I can reconnect next week and do something fun."

Pamela grinned at Houston. "Yeah, cousin, I'll bet you do have plans." She took a deep breath and said, "Okay, I'll go. Can you spare a few bucks for a room and maybe a meal or two?"

Parker reached for her purse. "I have a little money, and I can send you with food. I have some nice sandwich fixings and fruit—oh, and a frozen lasagna…"

Before she could continue, Houston lowered Olivia to the floor and dug into his pocket, pulling out a wad of cash. He peeled off three hundred-dollar bills and handed them to Pamela. "Here, will this help?"

Wide-eyed, Pamela grabbed the money, hopped down from the bar stool, and said, "It sure will. Thanks Houston." She picked up her purse and jacket and walked toward the door, calling, "I'll see you in a couple of days, Cousin Parker. Have fun, guys."

Parker stood stunned while she watched the woman she barely knew walk out the front door of her condo with a handful of Houston's money. She faced him and wailed, "What am I going to do? I don't want her staying with me. I don't even want her around for *one* night, let alone…I'm just too busy." She stomped her foot. "I have work to do. I can't be entertaining a virtual stranger. Houston, what do you think she has in mind?"

"I don't know," Houston said, "but, Parker, you're going to break that foot if you don't stop stomping it like that." When she began to carp again, he pulled her to him and kissed her. She relaxed in his arms until he suddenly pulled back and asked, "What's wrong with your cat?"

"What?" Parker asked, looking around for Olivia.

"I just saw her tear into the hall like something was after her. Is she having a fit? Does she have fits?"

"I don't know," Parker said, trotting into the hall calling, "Olivia! Olivia! Olivia, where are you?"

Houston followed her. "There," he said, pointing into the spare bedroom. "She's under the bed. I see her tail. She's agitated about something." He walked toward the cat and reached for her, but she bolted and skittered across the hall into Parker's bedroom.

"What is it, sweetie?" Parker asked, trying to catch up to Olivia. She pointed. "She went into the closet." Before Parker could react, however, Olivia ran out of the closet, down the hall, then tore around the living room a couple of times.

"Man, what do you think is wrong with her?" Houston asked, watching the cat with mounting angst.

"Gotcha," Parker said, finally catching up to Olivia. She sat down on the sofa with the cat and looked into her face. "What's wrong, baby girl?"

That's when Houston began to laugh. "There!" he said, walking closer. He pulled something off Olivia's fur and held it up. "It's one of those sticky notes." He grinned at the cat. "Did that little piece of paper attack you?"

"Poor thing," Parker said, smoothing Olivia's fur. "She does not get along well with sticky notes. I'm sorry, Olivia, if I left that where you like to sit."

"Where does she like to sit?" he asked.

"Everywhere," Parker said, laughing. She kissed the top of Olivia's head, then turned to Houston. "Okay, shall we have that beer, then how about dinner out and a concert?"

"A concert?" he questioned.

She smiled. "Yes. I could use a relaxing evening, and I'll bet you can too. There's a concert in a local park under the stars tonight." She ran her hand over his chest, kissed him, and crooned, "I thought we could take a blanket and a bottle of wine and…"

"I don't need a DUI, Babe, and neither do you. Let's make it iced tea."

She grinned impishly at him. "Our car arrives at six sharp. We have reservations at a classy place downtown, then we'll walk to the park for the concert, and our driver will pick us up when we're ready to come home." She kissed him. "Like it?"

"Yeah, I like it," he said, returning the kiss.

She pulled back and laughed. "I mean my plan. Do you like the plan?"

"Sure," he said, kissing her again. "Sounds good. A concert at the park. Why not? Yeah, a quiet evening together sounds terrific."

## Chapter Three

"This is nice," Parker said, later that evening as she and Houston sat together in the back of the ride-share car on their way to dinner.

"Yes, it is," he whispered, pulling her to him. "Thank heavens for the center seat belt."

She snuggled closer to him. "*No* seat belt would be even better."

Houston smiled and kissed her, then pulled back a little and asked, "So what's up with your cousin? I get the impression that you didn't know she was coming."

"I had no idea. I didn't even know she knew where I was staying. I guess she found out by snooping through Mom's things." She looked at him. "I don't know what in the heck I'm going to do with her if she insists on staying."

"Tell her no," he said matter-of-factly.

Parker winced. "She's really kind of fragile."

"She is?" he asked, disbelieving. "I thought she seemed kind of pushy, myself."

"Well, she's had a rough life, and she's just now coming back into *our* life—you know, the family. I don't want to reject her or make her feel like she's being rejected."

He grinned. "And what do you think you did this afternoon?"

"Yeah, I guess I wasn't very cordial, was I?" Parker agreed. "But, darn it, even family members need to respect each other's boundaries. Don't you think so?"

"Sure I do," Houston agreed.

She chuckled. "Spoken like a guy who has very few family ties." She added, "Well, we—you and I—have tonight and hopefully tomorrow. When are you expected in Texas?"

"I'll hit the road day after tomorrow."

Parker groaned.

"Here we are, folks," the driver said, pulling up in front of a group of restaurants. He stepped out of the car and opened the rear door for the couple. "Have a nice evening. Are you going to the concert after dinner?"

"Yes," Houston said. "Shall we call you when we're ready for a ride home?"

"Just call the service, they'll send a car."

Houston nodded. "Okay, thanks." He took Parker's hand and looked up and down the street. "There are a lot of restaurants. Where are we eating?"

"Where do you suggest? I have a reservation, but I don't mind ghosting them if you'd rather eat someplace else, like that Texas Smokin' Grill over there." Before he could speak, she said, "Or we could walk to that classier place up the street. See the lighted sign?" Before the couple took a step, someone bumped Parker, and she yelped.

"What happened?" Houston asked, steadying her. "Are you okay?"

"Yeah," she said, "but he almost got off with my purse. Did you see that? He grabbed my purse strap. When he realized it was attached to me—you know, across my shoulders, he let go and that's when I lost my balance."

"Which dude was it?" Houston asked, scanning the crowd.

She looked in the same direction. "I'm not sure. It happened so fast. All I know is he wasn't very big, and I think he was on roller skates or a skateboard."

"I doubt it," Houston said. "Otherwise he probably would have fallen."

Parker shrugged. "Well, I'm okay; let's go eat. I want to get a good spot at the concert."

"Are you sure that jacket will be warm enough to sit out on a night like this?" he asked.

She flashed him a smile. "What a thing to ask me, Houston. Where's your sense of chivalry? I was counting on you to keep me warm."

He wrapped an arm around her, leading her past the Texas Smokin' Grill and on down the street toward the classy restaurant with the lighted sign.

"Isn't this nice?" Parker asked later that night as the two of them sat on a grassy knoll listening to the music. She gazed up into the sky. "Even the stars are out tonight. And it's not that cold."

"No, it's nice," he said. "I especially like us relaxing together like this. I don't think either one of us has a lot of time to relax anymore."

She agreed. "Life seems to become more and more demanding."

"Are you getting tired of your work?" he asked.

"No," she was quick to say. "It's actually more interesting and exciting than ever. Never a dull moment, as they say."

"Good," he said, smiling. "I'm glad you're still living your dream, Babe." He pulled a bottle from Parker's tote bag and asked, "Want another swig of the wine?"

She nodded. "Yeah, I wouldn't mind another sip or two." She stood up. "After I visit the little girl's room."

"Want me to walk with you?" he asked.

"Escort me?" She questioned, grinning. She pointed. "It's right over there. It's well-lighted. I think I'll be just fine." She kissed him. "But thank you for offering."

"Hurry back," he said, lying down on the blanket and smiling up at the stars.

Parker also smiled as she walked toward the restroom. She stepped inside and looked around. *Nice,* she thought. *Big.* She opened the door to a cubicle when someone pushed in front of her. "Hey, what's your problem?" she complained, catching her balance and swinging around to get a look at who had detained her. "What do you want?" she asked, staring into the brown eyes of a woman wearing a hooded cloak and a veil.

"Effie wants you and the old man to back off," the woman said.

"Who are you?" Parker asked. "Who's Effie? I don't know what you're talking about." She pushed past the veiled woman. "Listen, I think you should get out of here and let me use the restroom."

"A gutsy one, huh?" a second cloaked and veiled woman said, walking closer to Parker.

"Back off, lady or I'll…" Parker snarled.

"You'll what?" the first woman challenged, reaching out a hand to block Parker. "Not until you hear what we have to say."

"What?" she snapped impatiently, looking down at the woman's hand which was wrapped around her wrist. *What is that?* Parker wondered. *It's kind of a brash tattoo for such a feminine hand. It looks like a sword with the face of a cat. Hmmm,*

*I wonder what that signifies.* She looked at the hand of the smaller woman. *She has it too. Maybe they belong to a cult—it's cult-like. And it relates to me how?* she wondered. She asked, "Okay, tell me, who's Effie and what am I supposed to stop doing?"

"Just stay away from Lake Drive. Leave the neighbors alone," the brown-eyed woman said, turning and running out of the restroom. The smaller woman followed at the same pace.

Parker hurried to the door and looked in the direction the women ran until they blended with the darkness and were no longer visible. *What in the heck?* she thought. *Lake Drive? This nonsense must be related to Jud's search for Hannah. Well, wait until I tell him about this strange encounter.* She stepped back into the restroom and entered the cubicle.

Minutes later when she stood at a sink washing her hands, she looked at herself in the mirror and jumped. *Who's that?* she wondered. She turned and found herself looking into the face of another veiled woman—a younger woman. "Who are you?" she asked.

"I…" the woman started. She winced, then ran out the door into the night. Parker took a breath and blew it out, then continued to rinse the soap from her hands. When she took another look in the mirror, she gasped. Behind her on a stall door was a large depiction of the emblem she'd seen on the women's hands. Parker stared at it for a few seconds, then hurried out of the restroom without stopping to dry her hands.

"Are you okay?" Houston asked when Parker dropped to her knees next to him. He gripped her shoulders and looked into her face. "What happened? You look like you've seen a ghost."

"Don't say that!" she insisted.

"What's wrong?"

"Houston, that's what it felt like…"

"What?" he asked impatiently.

"That I saw ghosts or ghouls or—I don't know what—three brides of Frankenstein, maybe."

"What are you talking about? In the restroom?" He looked in the direction she'd come from. "I don't see anything."

"They ran off."

"Three ghouls?" he repeated. "Parker, maybe you shouldn't have that second glass of wine."

She looked him in the eyes. "Houston, they were as real as you are. I felt them."

"You felt them?" he asked.

"One of them touched me twice, and she threatened me." Parker continued to babble, "They had these strange emblems on their hands—anyway, two of them did."

"A woman touched you?" Houston asked. "How? Were you assaulted?"

"She grabbed my wrist and told me to stay away from a certain neighborhood or else," Parker said.

"Oh, Babe, it sounds like a prank—you know, high school girls acting on a dare, trying to get a rise out of people. They're probably on their way home now laughing about having scared you." As she thought about what Houston had said, he took her hand. "Now come on and lie down here with me. The stars are amazing tonight, and the music is about to start again. Come on," he urged.

"Thank you," Houston whispered into Parker's ear on their ride home later that evening.

"For what?" Parker asked.

"For the really fun date. You did a good job of planning it. I had a great time. Even the weather cooperated."

She squeezed his hand. "I'm glad you had a nice time. I did too."

"Now for dessert," he whispered into her neck.

Their driver stopped in front of Parker's condo and got out. He hopped up onto the curb and opened the door for the couple. Parker smiled. "Thank you," she said. "It was nice of you to come back for us."

"Had to," the driver said.

She tilted her head. "Oh?"

He handed her a purple parchment envelope. "I had to give you this. Good night now," he said, quickly climbing back into the car.

"Wait!" Parker called, once she'd opened the envelope, but he had already driven away. "Dang," she said, stomping her foot.

"Would you stop that!" Houston insisted. "I swear you're going to hurt yourself."

Parker grinned. "That's what Wade said at Christmastime when I got so frustrated after that policeman took Olivia."

"Yeah, you were going to tell me about that…" he started.

"Not now, Houston," she said, obviously distracted by what she held in her hand. "Look at this," she insisted.

"What is it?" he asked, taking the envelope from her.

"Remember I told you those gals who assaulted me in the restroom had something tattooed on their hands—a cross and a cat—then one of those designs appeared on a bathroom door. It just appeared all by itself. Houston, that was so creepy. And now here it is on this purple paper."

"Oh, hon, someone probably used that paint that goes on invisible. People use it all the time in magic shows."

"But why?" Parker asked, not expecting an answer. "Why would someone threaten me like that and then do magic on the bathroom door?" She held up the envelope. "And why would our driver give me a piece of paper with that very same emblem of the cat and the sword? What does it mean?"

Houston moaned. "I guess it means you'll be doing some internet research before you come to bed tonight."

"You got that right," Parker asserted. She put the condo key into the lock, then pulled back and hissed, "Houston, did I forget to lock the door when we left?"

"I don't know, did you? I guess if it's open you did. Come on. It's getting chilly. Let's go inside and warm up." He put his arms around her from behind, scooted inside with her, and closed the door behind them. He started to pick her up and carry her into the bedroom, when they heard a voice.

"Hi, guys."

Parker recoiled and moved behind Houston.

"Who is it?" he called, flipping on a light switch. "Pamela?" he questioned.

"Pamela, what are you doing here?" Parker asked. "I thought…"

"I know, Par-Par," she whined, "I couldn't find a room, and I knew you had food here. I made a turkey sandwich and ate an apple and some of those cookies you had in the cupboard. I hope you don't mind." She whined, "I had nowhere else to go—absolutely no options."

Parker bit her lip to keep from saying what she wanted to say. Instead, she took a deep breath. "Yeah, okay. I guess we'll make do."

"Thank you," Pamela said, visibly relaxing. She asked more brightly, "Did you two have a good time?" She looked at Houston. "By the way, I used most of the money you gave me for a tank of gas and a couple of new outfits."

"You went shopping?" Parker asked, disbelieving.

"Yeah, I'll need clothes to apply for jobs."

"Here?" Parker asked. "You think you're going to live here? Pamela…" she started.

"By the way, I can't find your cat," Pamela declared.

"Olivia?" Parker screeched, panicked. "Olivia!" she called, walking through the condo, and looking in places where the cat was known to hide.

"I looked everywhere already," Pamela said.

"In my bedroom closet?" Parker asked, her voice shrill. "Drawers, cupboards?"

"Well, no," Pamela said. "I didn't know cats hide like that." She followed Parker through the house, finally saying more quietly, "Par-Par, there's the chance, although ever-so slight that…"

Parker spun around and faced Pamela with her hands on her hips, and demanded, "What?"

When Pamela saw the mounting rage on her cousin's face, she said, "Now, Parker, I didn't do anything deliberately, you know. I mean, I was watching out for her and all. I'm just saying she might have sneaked out when I brought in my stuff." When Pamela saw Parker's face drop, she whined, "I'm sorry, but things happen. Cats are curious. Isn't that right? I've always heard that cats are curious. I can't help it. I didn't mean for her to get out."

"How did you get in here, anyway?" Parker asked, trying not to sound as incensed as she felt.

"Oh yeah, that," Pamela said. "I planned to just wait in my car until you got home, but I got cold. So I walked around the place and found an unlocked window. It was a piece of cake to remove the screen and open the window. You'd be easy to burglarize, Parker. No one saw me or anything."

Parker glared at her cousin, walked quickly to the front door, and flung it open. "Olivia!" she shouted. "Olivia!"

"Here kitty-kitty!" Pamela called, in an effort to be helpful.

Parker spun around and hissed, "Don't say that."

"Don't say what?" Pamela asked, taken aback.

More quietly Parker said, "Kitty-kitty. She doesn't like it when people say kitty-kitty."

"How do you know that?" Pamela asked.

"She won't come to you if she hears that," Parker insisted.

"Well, obviously, she isn't coming anyway, so what difference does it make?" Pamela reasoned.

Just then they heard another voice. "Oh, you're home."

"Flo," Parker said. She winced. "I'm so sorry. Did we wake you?"

Flo shook her head. "No. I've been watching and listening for you to come home. Are you looking for your beautiful girl?"

"Yes," Parker said anxiously. "Have you seen her?"

"I sure have," Flo said. "After tonight, most of the complex is acquainted with Olivia."

"Oh my gosh," Parker said, feeling a mix of relief and horror. "Where is she?"

"Safe. Let me just say she's safe, but I should prepare you," Flo warned.

"For what?" Parker asked, feeling an uncomfortable lump in her throat. "Oh no, Flo, what has happened?"

"Nothing awful. She's fine. Come on," Flo said. She started to walk away and asked, "Got your phone? You'll want a picture of this."

"I want to see," Pamela said, trotting after them. Houston trailed along as well. When Parker became aware that the others were following, she said, "Flo, this is my fiancé, Houston and my cousin, Pamela." She explained, "Flo manages the condo complex, and she's one of the wonderful ladies behind a very old and successful cat colony."

"Cat what?" Pamela asked.

Parker put her hand on her cousin's arm. "I'll explain it to you later."

"How did Olivia get out, anyway?" Flo asked. "She wasn't even wearing her harness." Parker looked at Pamela, who said, "It was an accident. I guess maybe I left a door open or something."

Flo leaned closer to Parker and said quietly, "She's not a cat person, huh?"

Parker shook her head. "So where did you find her?" she asked.

Flo explained, "Well, I guess your beautiful girl heard activity around the pool. Beverly's children were splashing in the hot tub when they thought they saw an unfamiliar cat in the bushes. They wrapped up in towels and went exploring, but couldn't find anything. So Beverly herded the children back to their condo to get ready for bed. She was reading to the kids when they heard a loud meow, then another." Flo laughed and added, "A high-pitched meow like they'd never heard before. Well, little Liam and Emma put their faces up against the window and saw Olivia staring back at them from outside their patio door." Flo giggled as they walked. "I guess their first words were, "Can we keep her, Mommy? Can we keep her?"

"So she's having a sleepover with a couple of children?" Houston asked. "Way cool."

Flo shook her head. "No. When they went outside to get her, she skittered off. Meanwhile, Beverly called me to see if I knew where she belonged. I was pretty sure the cat she described was Olivia, except that I couldn't imagine how she would get loose like that. So while Beverly was putting her children to bed, her husband, Joel, came out to see if he could help me find her. We couldn't find her anywhere, and I sure didn't want to give up, especially if that was Olivia. So I began knocking on doors." She winced. "I even woke up a few people, but I figured it was worth it—Olivia is worth it."

"Why didn't you call me?" Parker asked.

"You told me earlier that you had a date." Flo glanced at Houston and grinned. "I didn't want to bother you and I saw no need to. I was convinced that we would find her. I just hoped it would be sooner rather than later."

"So where was she?" Pamela asked.

"Well, when Joel and I knocked on Mrs. Rand's door she said she'd been hearing what she thought was a chipmunk. She was glad we'd come by, because she was sure she had a chipmunk stuck someplace in her kitchen." Flo put her hand on Parker's arm and laughed. "I remember you once telling me about Olivia screeching like a banshee, and I thought maybe that's what poor Mrs. Rand was hearing—Olivia in distress. So we went inside and sure enough what we heard was a cat, all right. It wasn't coming from inside anywhere, so we went out her back door, and I called for Olivia. Of course, the noise stopped. I shushed the others and that's when the sound started up again. It didn't take us long to pinpoint her whereabouts."

"It was Olivia?" Parker asked anxiously.

"It sure was," Flo said. "She'd evidently crawled into Mrs. Rand's trash barrel where one of those pick-up mechanisms on a big trash truck had punched a hole in the plastic. We think that's how she got in there. Well, evidently before she could crawl back out, Mrs. Rand tossed a bag of trash in and that blocked the escape hole for your little scavenger."

"Oh, poor Livvie," Parker moaned.

"That's not the worst of it," Flo said. "She tossed in a filter full of coffee grounds, and it appears they landed right on top of your dear cat."

"Ohhh," Parker moaned, "but it could have been worse. It could have been chicken drippings or something greasy like that."

Flo cringed. "Well, it's a good thing she likes her bath, because I'm afraid something like that did come down on her. The next thing Mrs. Rand tossed in there was leftover stew." She nodded. "Yeah, she was cleaning out her refrigerator."

"Oh no," Parker moaned.

"Well, it gave Olivia something to eat, anyway," Houston quipped.

"So where is she?" Parker asked. "It sounds like she needs a bath."

Flo shook her head. "Helen and I bathed her."

"Helen?" Parker questioned.

"In number twelve. She came out to see what all the commotion was about, and she volunteered to bathe Olivia. She helps out at a local cat shelter and is accustomed to bathing cats."

"So she offered to do it after hours?" Parker asked. "I'll have to send her flowers or something." She put her hand on Flo's arm. "And I'll take you out to lunch. You're a lifesaver."

"Well, we sure didn't want to leave Olivia to her own devices with all that garbage on her. No. We needed to get that off her."

"So is she at Helen's place?" Parker asked. "Should I go get a towel to wrap her in so she doesn't get a chill?"

"Oh no," Flo said. "Helen and I used a hair dryer on her. She's back to beautiful—just still a little smelly. The coffee and the stew spices didn't mix well with the shampoo Helen used. But the scent will wear off. Olivia will have her own kitty-cat aroma soon."

"Well, then," Parker said, trying not to sound overly anxious, "where is she? I'd like to take her home and get some sleep."

"Okay, but they wanted me to bring you in this way so you can see your sweet-sweet girl," Flo said, quietly opening a gate. She led the others onto a patio, waved at a woman through the window, and pointed into the house. "Is that cute or what?"

"Oh, Olivia," Parker muttered, smiling. "How precious." She looked questioningly at Flo.

"Helen and George are babysitting their granddaughter," Flo explained quietly. "They were having trouble getting little Hazel to sleep. Well, while Helen and I were cleaning up after the bath, I guess Olivia heard the baby crying, and she wandered into the room where George was trying to calm her. Hazel saw the cat, and she immediately stopped fussing and began cooing. Before George knew it, Hazel had calmed down enough that he was able to tuck her into the cradle. Olivia jumped in and lay next to her, and, look at that, George rocked them both to sleep." She clasped her hands under her chin. "Isn't that just the most adorable picture?"

Helen opened the sliding door and invited the others inside. "Hi," she said quietly. "I'm Helen." She looked at each of her guests. Who's the owner of this wonderful cat?"

"She's *my* girl," Parker said.

Helen chuckled. "I kind of hoped no one would claim her. She's an amazing babysitter. Heaven knows she saved my nerves tonight. I didn't think we'd ever get Hazel to sleep."

Parker smiled. "Olivia has that effect on babies and the elderly."

"She's a certified therapy cat, isn't she?" Flo whispered.

"I'm not surprised," Helen said. She frowned. "What was she doing out roaming around, anyway?"

Parker glanced at Pamela and said, "I guess she saw an opportunity and took it, the little scamp."

"Well, I hope we can remove her from the cradle without disturbing Hazel," George whispered. He pointed. "Oh, look! The cat just woke up. She must have heard your voice."

"Job completed, huh, Olivia?" Houston whispered, running his hand over her fur. He picked her up. "Ready to go home? You can put *me* to bed now."

Everyone tittered quietly.

"Thank you ever so much for taking care of her this evening," Parker said as they walked Flo back to her condo. She chuckled. "And thanks for bathing her. She looks great."

"She smells a little like coffee, though," Houston said, still holding her in his arms.

Flo winced. "We did our best to get the smells out."

"She smells good," he said, taking another whiff of Olivia's fur.

Two mornings later, Parker walked into the kitchen with Olivia trotting along beside her, and she heard Pamela's cheery voice. "Coffee's ready. Want me to pour you a cup?"

"Good morning, Pamela," Parker said without much enthusiasm. She then said, "Coffee? Thank you." She opened the refrigerator.

"I have breakfast under control," Pamela said. "You don't even have to think about what to fix this morning."

Parker yawned. "Oh, well, I was just getting Olivia's food." She closed the door and asked, "You've fixed breakfast?"

"Yes. I have an egg and sausage casserole ready to put into the oven as soon as everyone's ready. I found eggs and sausage and cheese and bread. I can make a mean breakfast casserole with those ingredients. Oh, and milk. Yeah, I think you'll like it."

"You found sausage?" Parker asked.

Pamela nodded. "In the freezer. I thawed it in the microwave. I hope that was okay."

"Yes," Parker said, surprised. "Sounds good." She looked suspiciously at her cousin. "What's the occasion?"

"I just want to be helpful," Pamela explained. "And since Houston's leaving today, I thought he'd want a stick-to-your-ribs type breakfast before he goes." She brightened. "What are you doing today, Parker? Want to hang out? We could go shopping." She frowned. "Why are you watching the cat like that?"

"Just waiting to see if she's going to eat," Parker said. "She can be a cranky-pants eater. Watch," she suggested. "See, first she ignores her plate. Then she sort of sneaks up on it when she thinks I'm not looking."

Pamela chuckled. "Yeah, she looks wary. Why is that? I've heard that cats can be finicky."

"Sure, there are finicky cats, then there's Olivia." She continued with her commentary. "See how she sniffs it? She may even lick it, then, yup, there she goes walking away from her delicious breakfast."

"Can't you make her eat it?" Pamela asked

"You can lead a cat to food, Pamela, but you can't make her eat it. No, I used to follow her around with the plate, beg her to eat, pretend I was eating it and tell her how yummy it is, and I got nothing. She wouldn't even look at me."

Pamela laughed. "You pretended to eat cat food?"

Parker nodded. "Yes. That actually works with some cats."

Pamela stared down at Olivia. "So she's not just a finicky eater?"

"Not really," Parker said. "I think it's more than being finicky. It's almost like a game she plays with me. She knows I want her to eat, and she's not going to give me the satisfaction."

"Is Olivia using psychology on you again?" Houston asked, walking into the room.

"Yeah," Parker said, chuckling. "I guess that *is* what she's doing."

"So is she going to eat that?" Pamela asked, continuing to focus on the cat.

"Yeah, probably," Parker said, "but she'll wait until I'm not looking. And it's more like she inhales it, rather than eating it." She wrapped her arms around Houston and gave him a quick kiss. "Hungry?" she asked. "Pamela has fixed us some breakfast." She poured him a cup of coffee and the two of them sat down at the bar counter and watched Pamela put the casserole into the oven.

"So," Pamela said, joining them at the counter, "want to hang out with me today, Parker, and show me the area?"

"I'm meeting someone this morning," Parker explained. "Olivia and I'll be gone for most of the day."

104

"Doing what?" Pamela asked.

Parker thought about how to respond, finally saying, "I'm involved in an investigation."

"Oh," Pamela chirped. "Can I tag along? I'm bored. I got so bored yesterday while you and Houston were gone. And her," Pamela said, nodding toward Olivia. "I don't know why you took the cat with you. You can trust me. I sure wasn't going to let her get out again."

"I often take her with me," Parker said. "It was no big deal."

"No big deal?" Houston repeated. He looked across the counter at Olivia when she jumped up into the chair next to Pamela. "There you are, you little troublemaker," he said.

"Troublemaker?" Parker spat. "She was not a troublemaker yesterday. In fact, she was a good girl. She was on her best behavior for you, Houston." Parker tilted her head. "What did she do that you thought was so naughty?"

"She took a bite of my burger when I wasn't looking," he complained.

Parker laughed. "Houston, when are you going to learn that you can't leave food unattended when there are animals around? Dogs, horses, and especially cats, will always take advantage of a situation like that."

"I just turned my back for a minute to toss that ball to those kids. Anyway, you were supposed to be watching her. Where were you when she attacked my burger?"

Parker thought for a moment and said, "I think that's about the time I received a text from one of my editors."

"What else did she do, Houston?" Pamela asked, amused.

"She climbed a tree and Parker made me go up after her."

"So you went to a park?" Pamela asked.

"Yeah," Houston said, "when you take a cat someplace you have to do everything outside—not that I mind being out of doors." He thought for a moment and said, "But taking a cat someplace is just a different experience. You tie up a horse and he stays tied and quiet until you come back, climb aboard, and nudge him to go someplace else. A cat either gets away from you or she pulls you around at the end of the leash and cries if she doesn't get her way."

"She cried?" Pamela asked.

"Well, yeah, in cat talk—you know *meow, meow*," he imitated.

"Only because she thought that woman needed her help," Parker said.

He laughed. "Oh, yes, the old woman who was planting flowers around that fountain."

Parker nodded. "You may have noticed she had a walker. Olivia knows about walkers." She chuckled. "She likes to ride on the trays of walkers when we visit nursing homes, and she knows to be careful around a walker."

Pamela laughed. "So the wheels don't roll over her tail or paw or something?"

"Sure," Parker said, "and so that she doesn't trip up the person. She seems to have respect for walkers and the people who use them." She bounced in her seat. "Once she alerted us to a man who had fallen. There he was on the floor, his walker overturned. She knew something was wrong and came to get us right away."

Houston chuckled. "She probably had something to do with the upset."

"Not according to the man," Parker insisted. "In fact, he showed us the small piece of Velcro on the floor that had stopped his walker wheels and caused him to fall. He even knew whose shoe it had broken off of. He admitted he was going too fast."

"Really?" Pamela said, staring curiously at Olivia. She asked, "So what happened with the lady who was gardening?"

Parker glanced at Houston. "Well, he's right. Olivia was carrying on something fierce, and she seemed to be trying to lead us to the lady. I think she was concerned because the woman wasn't using her walker. Olivia saw the walker to one side, and she saw the woman on her knees digging in the dirt."

"Do you mean she thought the woman had fallen? She can figure out things like that?" Pamela asked. "How does a cat do that? Can most cats do that?"

Parker shrugged. "I don't know, but Olivia was concerned, wasn't she, Houston?"

"I guess," he said. "Yeah, Pamela, when Parker took her over to where the woman was digging and planting, Olivia was all over the woman, pawing her and nudging her with her head."

Parker nodded, adding, "Then she'd sit down next to the woman and look up at me as if to say, 'Do something, Mom.'"

"And she didn't settle down until the woman stood up and took hold of her walker," Houston said.

"She's a funny cat," Pamela said.

Houston shook his head. "Not so funny when she gets rowdy and knocks down a little kid who was just minding his own business."

"Why did she do that?" Pamela asked.

"She may well have saved that little boy's life!" Parker exclaimed.

"Oh, come on," Houston said, grinning, "she was being a nuisance—a bully."

"Houston," Parker scolded, I told you that dog was growling at the little guy. The kid was trying to take the dog's bone away, and the dog was snarling. I'm afraid that if Olivia hadn't sidetracked the kid, things might have become ugly. Once the boy saw Olivia he forgot about the dog's bone."

"But did the cat have to knock the kid down?" he asked.

"All she did was rub up against his legs. He fell easily onto the soft grass."

Houston looked into Parker's eyes. "You have an excuse for everything she does, don't you?"

She grinned. "That's because there's usually a reason for the things Olivia does."

"Now you're telling me she has the capacity to reason?" he asked.

"I'm not sure about that," Parker said, "but cats have amazing instincts and senses. At least Olivia does." She sat up straighter, saying, "And did you know that cats can predict natural disasters and even diseases in people and other animals?"

He shook his head. "I can't and I won't believe that a cat—any cat—is smarter than my horse. I mean, you haven't taught her one trick, have you? Can she do tricks? My horse can."

"She doesn't do tricks and it's not because she can't." Parker grinned impishly. "It's because she doesn't want to."

Pamela laughed. "Do you two have this cat-versus-horse argument often?"

Parker looked at Houston for his response, then said, "It's not really an argument, just a difference of opinion. Houston hasn't yet accepted Olivia's superiority."

"Awww come on, Parker," he complained.

"Casserole's ready," Pamela said, taking it out of the oven and placing it on the counter. "Everyone back to their corners. Round two after breakfast."

"So, can I go with you?" Pamela asked after Houston had left and Parker prepared to leave for the day. "What sort of investigation is it, anyway? Something juicy? You write about crimes, don't you? What's this one about—murder, embezzlement, extortion, human trafficking…?"

"Human trafficking," Parker repeated. "That's an interesting concept." She thought for a moment, then responded, "It's a missing-person's case, basically. We don't know what else might be involved."

"Oh? So who are you meeting?" Pamela asked.

"A detective who actually has a personal interest in the case."

"When did this person go missing? What were the circumstances?" Pamela asked.

"It's all rather complicated." Parker sat down across from her cousin and asked, "What are your plans, Pamela? It sounds like you've quit your job."

"Kinda, sorta," Pamela admitted. "I've probably been fired by now. I just didn't go to work.

I think they got the message that I'm not coming back. I didn't like that job, anyway."

"Pamela," Parker scolded, "you need an income. You need to find a job you can commit to and stick with in order to build a career and a future. Don't you have any ambition or goals? What plans are you making for your future?"

When Pamela shrugged, Parker said, "Okay, where do you see yourself in ten years?"

"Dead," Pamela quipped.

"How morbid," Parker said. "How about five years? Think about it, where do you want to be in five years?"

"Seriously?" Pamela asked. When she saw that Parker was indeed serious, she responded. "Okay, in a museum."

Parker grinned. "As a relic, or are you saying you'd like to work in a museum?"

"I like being in that um—you know, around the things that are in a museum. Like I told your mom at Christmas, if I had to choose my favorite place to be all day, every day it would be in a museum. So if I also need to make money, then working in a museum would be my ideal job."

"Are there job opportunities in that area?" Parker asked.

"I don't know. All I've done so far is volunteer in a museum a time or two."

Parker looked at her cousin. "What's the appeal of a museum for you? I mean really? I can't imagine it."

"Well," Pamela started, "it's quiet and peaceful. Everything's organized. There's no chaos, and I like being around old things—you know, like some of the things in your mom's home and that our grandmother had in her home."

"So maybe it's your childhood memories that are taking you down that road," Parker said quietly.

Pamela shrugged again.

"You were safe then and happy when you lived with us. Is that what you feel when you spend time in a museum?" When Pamela didn't respond, Parker picked up her phone and tapped the screen a few times. "Let's see if there are any job listings anywhere for museum work." Surprised, she said, "Well, Pamela, there's quite a list of job openings right now. Did you know that? Have you actually looked at sites like this?"

"No," Pamela admitted. "I haven't taken the time. Hey, let me see that." After scrolling through the job listings, she said, "Gosh, I had no idea. There really are a lot—about a dozen of them—but where would I start?"

"I'd say by finding out the qualifications and requirements for each of the jobs that interest you. Decide where you'd like to live, maybe, and get to work preparing yourself with the credentials and schooling you would need."

Parker took her phone back, looked at the listings, and said, "For example, do you want to work inside or outside?

"Inside or outside?" Pamela questioned.

"In a regular museum inside a building, or at a sea-life museum on a pier, or an outdoor museum featuring gardens, for example, or butterflies or animals. There are a lot of different kinds of museums—aircraft, military, presidential…" When Pamela looked at her inquisitively, Parker said, "I did an article on museums once, and I know that there are a lot of different types of them—something for everyone. Their human resources people will be looking for employees with the right kind of education, but also someone with a lot of enthusiasm for the work who is self-motivated, energetic, and reliable. Pamela, a good work record is important too. No one wants to hire a flake—someone who would walk out on a job without giving notice. If you want a good job in a museum or in any other area or industry, I'd say you need to start today preparing yourself so that you're employable—so that someone wants you on their staff."

"How do I do that, Parker? I'm already a disaster of an employee. I've never had a good work record."

"How badly do you want this job?" When Pamela looked at her blankly, she added, "On a scale of one to ten, how badly? How important is it for you to actually build and create a future for yourself? Does it mean anything to you?"

"Do you mean without having to rely on a man? I've done a lot of that," Pamela admitted.

"And have you learned that the only way to a good relationship with a man is by becoming independent?" Parker offered.

"I guess I never learned any of that. I've been doing things all wrong. Well, Parker, I didn't have role models growing up. You and your mom are good role models, but I'm not you, and I don't know how to be you."

"That's good," Parker said. "You shouldn't try to be me or anyone else. You are unique, Pamela. You have something different to give to a job position, and it's time you found out what that is. It seems that first you need to believe in yourself—believe that you can do better—then strive to do better in everything you do each and every day."

"Oh," Pamela said. "That sounds familiar, only it makes more sense when you say it. Is that how you found your place, Parker—I mean your place in your career and in society?"

"Pretty much," Parker said, "along with taking risks. I'm kind of a risk-taker and maybe a rebel." She looked at her cousin. "You strike me as a bit of a rebel, but I think you're rebelling against the wrong things. You're getting in your own way a lot."

Pamela swooned. "Where have I heard that before?"

"Where?" Parker asked.

"In therapy." Pamela grinned. "So can I go with you today?"

Parker frowned. "And how would that further you on the road toward your five-year goal?"

"Research," Pamela blurted. "I could observe you in your environment doing your thing. I think I'd learn a lot about confidence and work ethic and…"

Parker grinned at her cousin. "Okay, you've sold me. Get your jacket and a pair of walking shoes, sunscreen, water bottle…" Parker picked up her phone and began texting. *Hi, Detective. We have a ride-along today. My cousin is in town, and she's interested in our work. I'm bringing her with me.*

She wasn't surprised at the response. *Oh great. First a cat and now a busybody tag-along. Parker, what are you thinking?*

She texted back, *I'll make sure she stays out of the way.*

*And the cat?* he quizzed.

*I can't make any promises about Olivia. LOL.*

## Chapter Four

"Where are we meeting the detective?" Pamela asked once they were in the car. "Who is he? Why are you working with him instead of the local police department? Who's the missing person, anyone you know? Why would you take your cat on an investigation, anyway? Isn't that a bit unprofessional?"

"Just watch and listen," Parker suggested. After a while she pointed. "There's the detective walking into the café." She mumbled, "I wonder if Lydia is working this morning."

Pamela leaned forward and squinted. "Hey, he isn't half bad looking. Is he married? How old is he?"

"He's widowed," Parker said. "I'd say he's in his mid to late fifties."

"He's cute in a rugged sort of way," Pamela observed.

"Are you looking?" Parker asked.

"Of course, I'm looking. I'm single aren't I?"

Parker spoke more sternly. "Well, keep a lid on it, will you? We have work to do today."

"Yeah, sure," Pamela said. "Hey, fix it so I'm sitting across from him, okay? That's better positioning than next to each other—you know, for conversation." She pulled down the sun visor and checked her reflection in the mirror. "Do I look all right?"

Parker shook her head in bewilderment.

"Well, hello Mr. Caldwell and Parker," Lydia greeted several minutes later when she brought menus to their patio table. Nice to see you again." She glanced at Pamela.

"This is my cousin, Pamela," Parker said.

Lydia nodded, then smiled. "I see you have your pretty cat with you this morning."

"She doesn't leave home without her," Pamela quipped.

"She's right," Parker confirmed, "but Olivia left home without me last night."

"She did?" Jud asked.

Pamela cringed. "I accidentally let her out when I sneaked in through a window." When she had the detective's attention she grinned coyly and said, "My bad."

Jud stared at Pamela for a moment, then asked their server, "Lydia, can you take a break in the next thirty minutes or so? I have a few more questions you might be able to answer."

Lydia glanced around, then said, "Yeah, let me take your order and bring your food. I should be able to break away before you're ready to leave."

"Good enough," Jud said. He asked, "Got your order pad ready? I know what I want."

"Don't need a pad," Lydia said. "I keep it in my head. What can I get for you?"

"A two-egg ham and cheese omelet, no potatoes, English muffin, orange juice, and coffee."

"Okay, and for you ladies?" Lydia asked.

"Just coffee," Parker said.

Pamela grinned at Lydia. "How I wish I hadn't already eaten breakfast. I'd love to order a whole lot of things and see if you can get it right." When Lydia gazed at her without responding, Pamela said, "Coffee, please."

Parker frowned at her cousin, watched Lydia pour their coffee, then reached into her purse, removed an envelope, and handed it to Jud.

"What's this," he grumped, "your resignation letter?"

She shook her head. "It's something someone gave me a couple of nights ago under very unusual and distressing circumstances."

"What?" he asked, removing a piece of paper from the envelope.

"Wow!" Pamela said. "What a pretty shade of purple." She asked, "Yeah, what happened the other night? You didn't tell me anything about that."

Parker glanced at her cousin, then explained to Jud, "I was assaulted—or maybe you'd say detained—by two women, although I guess there were actually three in the restroom."

"In a restroom?" Jud asked.

"Yes, at a park. Houston and I went to a concert. These women evidently stopped our driver and asked him to give this to me. At least two of the women had this emblem drawn on the back of their hands."

"So they were tattoos?" Jud asked.

"Probably," she said.

"And you think this is of interest to me because…?" he egged.

"Jud, they told me to stay off Lake Drive and out of that neighborhood. They gave me a warning and maybe a threat."

His interest now sparked, Jud looked more closely at the emblem. "What do you think it means?" he asked.

Parker hesitated before saying, "I think it means that whoever has Hannah wants to keep her, and they don't want us snooping around."

He muttered, "Most likely. So she *is* being held under duress and against her will."

"Wow!" Pamela blurted. "The plot thickens." She leaned forward. "Who's Hannah?"

Parker hissed, "Pamela, you're just along for the ride. We'll give you information on an as-needed basis."

"Okay," Pamela said, "but I can tell you right now that you're dealing with something outside the norm." She leaned closer and said more quietly, "You know—witchcraft, voodoo—maybe something evil."

"Why do you say that?" Parker asked.

"Let me see that thing close up, will you?" Pamela said, reaching for the emblem.

Jud handed it to her and asked, "Have you seen this before? Do you know what it means or where it came from?"

Just then Lydia delivered Jud's meal. He sat back so she could place it in front of him. "Will there be anything else?" she asked. He shook his head, and she said more quietly, "You go ahead and eat. I'll join you in ten or fifteen minutes."

Parker watched Jud salt and pepper his omelet and pour a little salsa over it, then she asked her cousin, "So, have you seen that symbol before?"

"Sure I have," Pamela said. "Among my vast array of experiences and adventures and shortfalls, I've dabbled in spiritualism and mysticism."

"Why am I not surprised?" Parker quipped.

Pamela flashed a grin at her, then spoke more quietly. "Along with that sort of journey, you sometimes find yourself involved in a random witchcraft ritual. Well, there was a period in my life when I thought it was all rather fascinating. I even collected the symbols that different sects created."

"Are you saying there are different branches of that weirdo magic-spell stuff?" Jud asked. "Are they organized and competitive? Would you say there's competition among them?"

"I don't know if you'd call it competition," Pamela said, "but they do each have their identifying marks and their own ways of doing things." She thought for a moment, then said, "Some of them are more dangerous than others, especially those who don't know what they're doing."

"Wow!" Parker exclaimed. "Pamela I didn't know you had knowledge of that world—the world of hexes and devil worship and..."

"Glad you brought me along?" she asked, grinning.

"Sure," Parker said. She looked suspiciously at Pamela and asked, "Now, this is valid information, right? You aren't fabricating."

"Look it up," Pamela insisted. "Yes, I know what I'm talking about."

"So are you familiar with the group that uses this symbol—a sword with a cat?" Parker asked.

"Not personally," Pamela said, "but I've heard of them. I've seen the symbol, and I know they gather up in this area. They have a very hush-hush, hoity-toity thing going on—you know, exclusive. I'm not sure how true it is, but I've heard this is actually an older cult. They recently reorganized. Now they cater to the elite. Their leader is an older woman named Effie; I don't actually know if she's still alive. Others may have taken over using her position and her name by now."

"Effie?" Parker blurted. She slapped her hand over her mouth and glanced around, hoping no one had heard her outburst. She leaned toward Jud and said more quietly, "They told me to watch out for Effie."

"Who?" Jud demanded. "Who told you that?"

"Those women in the restroom," she hissed.

Jud sat back and shook his head. "No, no, no," he muttered. "Not something unearthly. I can deal with thugs, ne'er-do-wells, downright idiots, but something from beyond common sense, the unnatural stuff people make up out of a boiling pot of nonsense, no! Don't take me down that path, please."

Parker and Pamela rolled their eyes at one another, and Parker checked on Olivia. She ran her hand over the cat's fur as she lay on a chair next to her, then she said, "Pamela, so tell me about some of your mystical experiences. What sort of rituals have you been involved in? Do you recall anyone being kidnapped and held hostage in any of those sects or cults or whatever?"

Pamela thought for a moment, then shook her head. "I don't think so, but I was never in the inner circle of a coven, so to speak." She brightened. "I have a lot of stories of the supernatural, though. Want to hear them? I mean, there was the time my friend Kyle lost a finger. I mean, he lost it and…"

"Not while I'm eating," Jud grumbled. When the two women looked at him, he said, "Why don't you girls go sit in the car if you want to talk about that baloney, or maybe you can schedule a fright night or something."

Parker chuckled. "Okay, if you're squeamish…"

"I'm not squeamish," he insisted. "I just don't want to hear fake tales from someone's wild imagination. That's what those psychics and crystal-ball readers use, you know—their own imagination." He pushed his plate away and took a swig of coffee just as Lydia returned to their table.

"I have ten minutes," she announced. "What more do you want to know?"

Jud pulled out a chair for her, and she sat down. "Do you know anything about this?" he asked, dropping the page with the strange symbol in front of her.

Lydia stared down at it. "Yes, I've seen it, but I don't know what it means."

"Where have you seen it?" Parker asked.

"Oh, here and there," she said. "It kind of gives me the heebie-jeebies. I don't really want to get involved. I see it and I ignore it. That's all."

Parker leaned forward. "What has you frightened?"

Lydia thought for a moment and said, "The implications, I guess." She glanced around suspiciously, then she continued quietly, "in a word, witchcraft or something of that ilk. That's the scuttlebutt. That stuff scares me, so I stay clear of talk about it or anything related to it." She added, "In fact, I'd rather not be sitting here looking at this right now." When she started to stand up Jud gripped her wrist.

"Please," he begged. He snatched up the emblem and tucked it away. When Lydia relaxed a little, he said, "Okay, let's go back to the topic of the Dunbar house."

Lydia gasped. "Why? Why did you say that? I didn't bring that up."

"No, you didn't," Jud said soothingly. "I did. I just want to know if you can give me a little history of the place."

"Well, the Dunbar family has owned that big old house for as long as I can remember. It used to be a five- or six-bedroom home and that's where the Dunbar family grew up—the original couple, Effie and Harold raised their two kids there. When he died back thirty-some years ago, she partitioned it off and made it into a two-family home—you know, a duplex." She leaned forward. "At least it wasn't turned into a boarding house for wayward kids, although there were young people living in there most of the time, and the elder Mrs. Dunbar continued to live in the house. She's the grandmother of the current bunch of kids—Brad, Travis, and others, and she was pretty much sequestered to the upstairs portion of that one side of the duplex. They installed stairs up to her quarters on the outside of the house, and folks around here were always surprised at the number of people climbing that staircase to visit Mrs. Dunbar. I guess she must have lived a private life upstairs without concern for what went on below her because she seemed to have a blind eye when it came to the condition of her grandsons' unit and all of the young people living in or maybe just hanging out there." She winced. "Or maybe she just didn't care anymore."

"So what are the names of the young people who lived there most recently?" Jud asked. "Would that be Brad and Travis?" He removed a pad and pencil from a pocket. "Are they brothers?"

"Cousins, I believe," Lydia said.

"Do you know the girls' names—I mean the girls you mentioned last time we talked? I'm particularly interested in those living there within the last ten years. What were their names?"

"Well, there was Veronica, Melanie, and Lucy, the young lady I showed you a picture of.

Lucy came within the last ten years. The others had been there longer." Lydia frowned. "I worried about those girls, you know. They just seemed lost somehow—like they didn't have a life of their own. It was all about Brad and Travis and maybe Mrs. Dunbar." She shook her head. "It's just an odd situation, if you ask me."

Jud thought for a moment, then asked, "Did the girls...the young women...stay with Brad and Travis when they left the house—you know, after the remodel?"

Lydia shook her head. "No one knows for sure if any of them left or if they're still living in that place." She smiled. "They did quite a job with that remodel, didn't they?"

Jud nodded. "It's something else all right, like someone plucked it from a hillside in England and dropped it in this unlikely setting." He turned in his chair to face her. "So do you know anyone who has seen the Dunbar kids or any of the girls around here since they remodeled that house?"

Lydia thought for a moment, then shook her head slowly. "Not that I know of. I just figured they moved on. It didn't matter one way or another to me or to most of the community, I don't think." She tilted her head and looked Jud in the eyes. "Why? What's your interest in the Dunbars and those girls? When we talked a few days ago—you know at my house, you seemed most interested in Lucy. Why?" she asked.

Jud glanced around, then spoke more quietly. "I believe that she is my daughter. She disappeared seven years ago without a trace."

Lydia gasped. "Well, no wonder you're so interested in that bunch."

"I knew it!" Pamela said. "Daughter, huh? Now this is really getting interesting."

Jud stared across the table at Pamela, then removed a picture from his pocket and showed it to Lydia. "Is this Lucy, the same girl in the newspaper photo you showed me?"

"Yes," she said. "Yes, I believe so. When was that picture taken? How old was she?"

"Seventeen," Jud said.

Lydia nodded. "Yes, that's Lucy, only…"

"Only?" he questioned.

"Only, she looks different somehow. There's more life in her in that picture. She always seemed…"

Parker asked, "Do you think she and the other girls were being held against their will in that old house?"

Lydia fidgeted nervously for a moment, then said, "The thought crossed my mind a time or two, but I actually saw no evidence of it, if you know what I mean. The girls seemed to have the freedom to leave and go about their business if they wanted to, but they didn't appear to want to. They always stayed close to the house. They never had much to say when they came into the café together, but you didn't see the young women out and about alone." She smiled. "Except for Lucy. I used to see her sitting on the porch with Virginia at her big Victorian house sometimes, but other than that, yeah, it was like they were sequestered to the Dunbar house—an unsocialized bunch, they were."

"And you don't know where they went?" Jud asked.

"Rumor has it that some of them are involved in the business, but your girl—no, I don't think she's still there, but then, I don't think anyone really knows who works there, who lives there, or even what goes on in that place. I haven't seen hide nor hair of the girls or the cats since they made the big changes."

"Cats?" Parker questioned.

"Oh yes, that girl—your girl, Lucy, was always sitting with the cats. They were mostly strays, you know. Some might have belonged to someone, but they were drawn to your girl, and she often sat sketching them. I used to wonder what she did with the drawings." Lydia tilted her head. "Like I said when you came to my house, Lucy seemed to live in her own small world. There just didn't seem to be much going on inside her head. She'd speak when spoken to. She'd smile, but there really wasn't much behind that smile, if you get my drift. I sometimes wonder…" She took a breath and looked at the detective. "Actually, I didn't know what to think, if she was just simple or what?"

"No," he said emphatically. "She was… what's the word?" He thought for a moment and said, "She was full of life and energy."

"Vibrant?" Parker suggested.

"Yes," Jud said. He frowned. "What did those people do to her?" No one spoke until Jud asked quietly, "Lydia, is there anyone else I can talk to who might know where that crowd went?"

"Well, there's the family. I told you that the family opened the business there."

"It's a dance studio?" he asked.

Lydia smirked. "If they're doing Zumba dance in there, I'm the Queen of England."

"So what do you think they're doing?" Jud asked.

"Well, yeah, they might be doing some dance classes, but I don't believe that's the actual draw to the place—you know, the attraction. People come from all over. Practically everyone who shows up there is from out of town and many from out of state and maybe out of the country. They don't stay here for long, but sometimes they'll come into the café, which as you can see is just about the only show in town. I can tell these are folks of a different caliber."

"Different caliber?" Parker questioned.

"Well, not that they're of a higher caliber," Lydia explained. "They're just a might different from the folks around here. For some reason they come here, spend time at the house of who-knows-what-goes-on-in-there, then they get back into their Humvees, Jaguars, and Mercedes and resume their lives elsewhere." She leaned forward. "I think it's witchcraft."

"Bingo," Pamela said.

Parker flashed a warning glance at Pamela, then asked, "Lydia, what makes you say that?"

The server glanced at her watch and stood up. "Hey, I need to get back to work. It's been nice chatting with you again."

"Lydia," Parker said, "you mentioned an older woman. Is she still on the property? Do you know if there are living quarters inside? Could she be living there?"

"I'm pretty sure there are people living in there, else wise, we'd see those Dunbar people here in town, and we don't—at least not so we'd recognize them." She glanced toward the restaurant entrance. "Hey, I'd better get back to work." She started to stand up, then leaned in and said quietly, "Since that place was refurbished, we sometimes see peasant people, at least that's what we call them. They're on bicycles and on foot. Rumor has it that they are some of the Dunbar family and maybe employees."

"So you don't recognize them when you see them?"

Lydia shook her head. "They stay hidden— you know, in shrouds. You can't tell one from the other." She giggled. "Except for one of them wears hot-pink shoes. You can see those bright pink shoes flashing from under her cloak as she rides her bicycle around town." Lydia stood up. "I've probably already said too much, but I hope it helps you in some way."

"Thank you, Lydia," Jud said, also standing up. He nodded to her as she walked away, then sat back down and turned to Parker. "Well, what did you get from all that?"

Flippantly, she said, "You have a name and maybe a direction."

"A direction?" he spat. "What direction?

She nodded to her left. "To the house of who-knows-what-goes-on-in-there." She brightened. "Let's go check it out, shall we?"

Wide-eyed, Pamela said, "Yeah, let's go. I love things like that."

"Wait," Jud said.

"What? Aren't you curious? I mean, they surely know where Brad and Travis took Hannah," Parker said.

"But…" he stalled.

"Uncle Jud," Parker whined, stomping both feet, "I want to do Zumba. Please sign me up for Zumba or ballroom dancing or whatever they do in that place, please, please." She grabbed Pamela's arm. "My cousin wants to dance, too, right, cuz?"

Jud frowned, confused, then he grinned. "Oh, I get it. You want to do the dance thing so you can…" He nodded. "Yes, favorite nieces of mine, let's go see about getting you some dance lessons." He started to stand up, then he leaned toward Parker. "I have to wonder, why didn't Virginia mention the outside staircase on the house and the—what did Lydia say—constant string of visitors? Wouldn't you think Virginia would have noticed that?"

Parker thought for a moment. "Well, she didn't seem to want to know what was going on there. Remember, she pulled her drapes so she couldn't see the Goth house. And she might be a tad forgetful. There are probably many things she has forgotten over the years because she didn't think they were important."

Jud nodded. "Yeah, you could be right. Okay, let's go," he said, pushing away from the table. He peered underneath it, and asked, "Parker, where's your cat?" He glanced around the patio. "Is she dining with strangers again?"

"What?" Parker blurted, looking under the table. She suddenly felt that familiar dread she always felt when Olivia wasn't where she expected her to be. "Olivia!" she called, quickly scanning the area.

"Shhh," Pamela said.

"You shush," Parker snapped, standing up for a better view of the patio area. She called again, only more quietly, "Olivia!"

Just then a gentleman sitting at a table with a large group of people waved to get her attention, "Ma'am, are you by any chance looking for a cat?"

"Yes," Parker said, walking closer to him. "Did you see where she went?"

"Not really," he said, "but I did see her when we came in." He motioned toward the others at the table. "As you can see, we have quite a group, and I think we may have startled the cat by our boisterous arrival."

"I noticed you come in," Parker said. "So what happened?"

"She's a tri-color cat, right—with a harness and dragging a leash?" the man asked.

Parker nodded. "That's her."

"I saw her walk across the patio toward the door," he reported. "No one seemed to be missing her, so I figured she was following her owner out. Then I became involved in the task of getting us seated and all, and I forgot about her."

A boy of about eight interrupted him. "Grandpa…"

"Not now, Bub," the man said. "You go ahead and make a move; I'll be right there." He turned back to Parker. "The boy loves to play those games on the placemats when we come here." He leaned closer to her and said quietly, "I almost always let him win. Sometimes he wins on his own. Kids are smart these days."

"Yeah," Parker said, impatiently. "My cat…" she started.

"Grandpa," the boy said again.

When the man waved the boy off a second time, a woman sitting across the table from him said, "Ed, listen to the lad. It's about the cat. I think he saw something."

Ed looked at the child. "What, Bub?"

"A lady put the cat in box on the back of her bike," the youngster said.

"What lady?" Parker asked.

The boy pointed. "I went out there with Mom to get her sweater out of the car, and I saw that scary bicycle lady put the cat in a box on her bike. The cat didn't want to go in there, but the lady pushed it in and closed the lid."

Parker walked up closer to the boy and squatted. "Where did she go, honey? Did you see which way the lady rode the bike?"

"I think it was broken," the boy said.

"Her bike was broken? So she didn't ride away?" Parker asked.

He shook his head.

An older boy laughed and said, "Someone probably let the air out of her tires. People do that all the time when they see those creepy bike people."

"Yeah," the eight-year-old said, "I saw her push the bike across the street to the gas station, probably to get air in her tires."

134

Parker stood up and trotted toward the exit, calling, "Thank you!"

Jud caught up to her. "Hey, where are you going?"

"Be right back," Parker said, running off the patio and around to the front of the café.

Jud and Pamela followed. When they caught up to Parker, Jud asked, "What's going on?"

"That boy saw someone with Olivia. She's on a bicycle—someone the boys say is kind of creepy. She put Olivia in a box on the back of her bike."

"There!" Pamela said, pointing to the left. "There's someone on a bike with a box on the back."

"Yes!" Parker shouted. "That must be her." When she realized that the cyclist had been slowed by traffic, she took off running, muttering, "I'll bet I can catch her, that thief."

"Wait!" Jud called, but Parker was on a mission and wasn't about to be deterred.

In that split second, Jud said to Pamela, "Let's head her off. "Quick," he shouted, "get in the car!"

Pamela yelped when Jud drove off even before she could close the door. She grabbed her seat belt and attempted to fasten it while Jud drove erratically down the street. "There!" she said, pointing. "The bike lady is stopped behind that bus.

Go around the block. Maybe we can catch up to her before Parker does."

Jud made a quick right turn and glanced at Pamela. "You've done this type of thing before, haven't you?"

She grinned at him and continued watching for the bicycle and for Parker. "There," she said as they rounded the corner going toward the bike rider and Parker, who was closing in on the cyclist. "Stop here," Pamela insisted. "I can head her off on foot. See that, Parker's only a little ways behind her. Let me out."

"Well, let me pull over and stop," he insisted.

"Yeah, sure," Pamela said, opening the car door.

"What are you doing?" Jud shouted, slamming on the brakes.

"Thanks," Pamela muttered, leaping out of the car. She darted into the street, dodging cars and working her way toward the other side, catching the attention of a patrol officer, who immediately made a u-turn and activated his siren.

Ignoring the warning, Pamela made it to the other side of the street and began running toward the woman on the bicycle. Then she heard the policeman call, "Stop right there, lady!"

Pamela glanced at him as he drove slowly alongside her. "I'll stop when we catch that thief!" she said. "She's on the black bicycle. Stop her!"

*What's she doing?* Parker thought when she saw Pamela running toward her on the sidewalk. She felt a surge of excitement. *Good, good, she's going to catch up to the catnapper before I can, but what's going on with that cop? It looks like he's after Pamela. No,* she thought. *No, let her go. We have to get Olivia back. Yeah, we're almost there.* Her thighs burned, as did her lungs. *I just hope one of us can reach the rider in time—before the traffic begins to move. Gadzooks, that cousin of mine can run. Great! If Pamela can stop her, I can catch up to them in time to help her detain the thief for that policeman. Oh, this is a lucky, lucky break.*

However, when she saw the traffic begin to flow, she panicked. *Oh no. We're not going to make it.* "Oh, Olivia," she moaned, and she began running faster. She was almost within tackling distance when the bicycle began to move with the traffic. "Wait!" she shouted. "Stop! You on the bicycle, stop!" Meanwhile, the policeman was driving slowly alongside the cyclist, but his focus was still on Pamela. "Officer," Parker shouted, "stop her. Stop the bicycle. She took my cat!"

Finally things seemed to register with the police officer, and he called out to the rider, "Can you stop your bike, ma'am? Pull it over to the curb, will you? Pull over to the curb."

The rider did as she was told and Pamela and Parker both converged on her. Pamela grabbed the woman, pulled her off the bike, and held her, allowing Parker to lift the lid on the box that was strapped to the back fender. "Empty," she said, slumping. She bent over, hands on her knees, trying to catch her breath.

The officer double-parked his car and joined the women on the sidewalk. He asked, "What's going on, ladies?"

"They accosted me," the cyclist said calmly. "They shouted at me, and chased me, and accosted me for no reason."

"She took my cat," Parker said. She screamed at the woman. "What did you do with my cat?"

"I have no cat," the cyclist insisted. "As you can see, I have no cat."

"Did you look in that box?" the officer asked.

"Yes," Parker said on the verge of tears. "All that's in there are groceries and books." She shouted, "What did you do with my cat? I want my cat back!"

"Oh, my God," Pamela shouted, pointing.

Parker looked up and gasped when she saw Jud walking toward them, cradling a fluffy calico cat. "Olivia!" she shouted, trotting toward him. "Where did you find her?" She took Olivia into her arms. "Where was she, Jud?"

"Well, while you girls were chasing down this poor innocent woman, I saw two more cloaked cyclist going in the opposite direction—one on

138

a green bike and the other on a black bike." He pointed. "…like that one. So I respected my suspicious nature, leaving you girls to fight your fight, and I followed bicycles numbers two and three. Doggone if I didn't see the lid on the green fender box lift a couple of times. I drove up closer, and saw two round eyes staring out at me. I don't know what happened to the black bike, but I was able to follow the green one to an herb shop. By the time I could park and approach the bike, which, by then, was chained outside the shop, Olivia had already escaped. There she was sitting next to the bike wondering which way to go. I scooped her up and here we are."

"Thank you, Jud," Parker said, giving him a one-armed hug. She held Olivia tightly and kissed her furry cheek. "Boy, am I glad to see you, sweet girl." She spoke into Olivia's fur, "So you had a wild ride on the back of a bicycle, did you? Poor baby."

"You found her," Pamela said, joining Parker and Jud. She looked into Olivia's eyes. "She really is a pretty cat."

Parker smiled. "Yes, she is." She put one hand on Pamela's arm. "Thank you."

"For what?" Pamela asked.

"For jumping into action to save her."

When Parker choked up, Pamela said, "You really do love her, don't you?"

Parker nodded. "Yes. Sorry, I'm kind of sappy about her."

Pamela thought for a moment, then said, "I don't think I've ever loved anyone or anything like that—at least not since I lived with you and your mom and dad. I sure did love all of you."

Parker put her arm around Pamela and held her for a moment. She pulled back. "Uh-oh, I think your cop friend wants to talk to you. Here he comes."

Pamela turned toward him and said, "Okay, give me a ticket or whatever you're going to do so we can be on our way."

"Well," he said, grinning. "I think we can overlook the infraction this time. We can't let citizens put themselves in danger running out into traffic like that, but we also can't stop them from trying to rescue a beautiful cat." He faced Parker. "So this is your cat?"

"Yes, and we thought that woman had her on her bicycle, but our friend," she pointed at Jud, "he spotted her on the back of another bicycle going in the opposite direction. Thank heavens."

The officer looked up and did a double take. "Jud?" he asked. He put out his hand. "Detective Judson Caldwell? I haven't seen you in, what—a year or so. Have you retired?"

Jud shook the officer's hand. "You might say that."

140

The officer looked at Parker and Pamela. "Well, it appears you're having a good time, surrounding yourself with beautiful women." He motioned toward the women. "Are you two sisters?"

Pamela put her arm around Parker. "Cousins."

"Well, you could be sisters," the officer said.

"Thank you," Pamela said, smiling. "So no ticket?" she asked, giving the officer her most convincing portrayal of innocence.

"Not this time, but…"

"I know, officer. Thank you. I won't do that again," Pamela said. "I promise."

"So the cat was kidnapped and riding around on another bicycle?" the officer asked.

Jud nodded then asked, "So, Klint, who are those cloaked cyclists, anyway? We don't see those in our neck of the woods."

"Yeah," Officer Klint said, "they're associated with the monstrosity of a damn resort or whatever that place is on Lake Drive. We've been trying to get a handle on what's going on in that place. I guess catnapping is one of their activities." He shook his head. "That won't bode well for them if they want to stay under the radar."

"No, it sure won't," Jud said.

The officer asked, "So, Jud, can you give me any sort of identifying marks for the cyclist you took the cat from?"

"I didn't take the cat from her. I followed the rider and saw the cat trying to get out of the box…"

"Gads," Parker said. "That would have been horrible if Olivia had jumped out into traffic." She closed her eyes and hugged the calico. "Just awful."

"So you stopped her?" Officer Klint asked.

"No," Jud said. "The rider stopped, chained up the bicycle outside that herb store across the main drag, and Olivia jumped out of there on her own. I took off with her while the gal was still in the store. As for an identifying mark," he thought for a moment, "no. I just saw her from the back." He pointed at the other cyclist and said, "She looked like an exact replica of that gal, only maybe a little smaller—oh, but the other cyclist I was following at the same time…"

"There were two of them?" the officer asked.

"Yes, but she rode on past the herb shop. I lost sight of her in traffic, but there was something," he said.

"What?" Officer Klint asked.

"Pink shoes."

"Pink shoes?" the officer repeated.

Jud nodded, "She was wearing pink shoes. I could see flashes of pink as she pedaled the bike."

The officer looked from one to the other of them and repeated, "Pink?" he looked down at the cyclist's shoes and asked, "Do you all wear black shoes, like those?"

"What are you talking about?" the young woman asked. "All of who?"

"You know what I mean. There's a society of you or something—a clan," the officer said.

The young woman shook her head. "I'm just out for a bike ride this morning—minding my own business. I don't know about someone with pink shoes. Can I go now?"

"Yeah, I guess," Klint said. He looked at Parker. "Do you want to apologize for your actions?"

She and Pamela looked at each other, turned, and walked away toward Jud's car.

## Chapter Five

"I must say that the Dunbar family did an amazing job of renovating this place." Parker said. "You'd never recognize it from that photo you have, Jud, except for the dramatic Goth architecture." She spun around, trying to take it all in. "The grounds are spectacular."

"Like an oasis on the edge of a tumbledown town," Jud said.

"It sure doesn't look like it belongs in this neighborhood," Pamela agreed. "I guess that's why they created a sort of world-apart feeling with that giant wall."

Parker grinned. "Pamela, you and Jud are both spewing poetry today."

Ignoring her, Jud said, "I wonder where they got their money."

"You said someone told you it's old family money," Parker reminded him.

Jud nodded. "Yeah, but from where—a gold strike, boot-legging, a legitimate business venture?"

"I wonder how long have they been sitting on it," Parker said.

"They did build that original Goth house. That must have cost a pretty penny even back in the day," Jud said.

"Well, let's go inside and see what we can find out," Parker suggested, picking up Olivia and walking up a series of wide steps to the covered porch." She stopped and looked around at the ominous canopied chairs placed strategically around the porch. She muttered, "For seclusion, I guess." She strained to see if any of them were occupied and by whom.

"Seclusion?" Jud questioned.

Parker nodded. "They seem to be designed for private meditation or…"

Just then Jud bristled. "What was that?" he asked, peering suspiciously into the distance.

"What?" Parker asked.

Pamela stiffened and glanced around. "I don't see anything."

"I guess it was a cat." Jud chuckled. "Look, it got your cat's attention." He tickled Olivia under the chin. "Did you see that pussycat?" He scoured the area again. "I sure thought I saw something or someone disappear into the shrubbery with a cat."

"Something?" Parker asked, gazing in the same direction.

"Yes," he confirmed. "It was like an apparition, if you believe in that sort of thing." He shook his head. "Weird."

"Well, shall we, Uncle Jud?" Parker said, taking his arm. She snuggled with Olivia and said into her fur, "Now you be a good girl." She smirked playfully at Pamela. "You too."

They all chuckled when Olivia mewed.

"She's been good today," Jud said. "A big help, in fact."

"Who," Parker quipped, "Olivia or Pamela?"

Pamela was quick to say, "Olivia ran away, remember, and got herself catnapped?"

Parker nudged her cousin. "Yeah, you only ran out into traffic and almost got a ticket." She winced, "Or worse."

Pamela fired back, "Did you want that woman to get away with your cat?"

"Yeah," Jud said, grinning, "but she didn't have the cat. You ambushed an innocent woman." He gazed around the courtyard again and mumbled, "Criminy, I can't believe I'm in the same country, let alone the same zip code."

"It *is* exotic, isn't it?" Parker said, lowering a wriggling Olivia to the porch and holding firmly to her leash.

"Exotic in an eerie sort of way," Pamela said. "I expect to see wolves and warlocks." She recoiled. "Do we really want to do this?"

"What's wrong?" Parker hissed. "I thought you liked adventure and mysticism."

"Not when it involves spells and eyeball stew," Pamela whispered.

146

Parker tried to control her urge to laugh.

"Don't do that," Pamela said.

"What?" Parker asked.

"Make a spectacle. You're making a spectacle."

Pamela started to turn away, and Parker grabbed her arm. "No, you don't. We're doing this together." When she felt Olivia tug against the leash, she picked her up. "No exploring on your own, Livvie. Sorry, sweetie."

"Well, there doesn't seem to be anything stopping us from going inside," Jud said, approaching the door. "Let's go."

The trio walked cautiously into a spacious foyer. They stopped and looked around when they heard a voice ask, "May I help you?"

They turned to see a woman with bleached-blond hair pulled back into a severe bun. Her eyes were boldly outlined in black. Before anyone could speak, her face softened into a smile. "What a pretty kitty. She's so colorful and all in the right shades."

"The right shades?" Parker questioned.

"Yes, she has orange—that gorgeous orange of emotion; the glorious black, which is power, strength, even seduction; and white, which balances it all out with the innocence living in each of us."

"Oh," Parker said, "I've never heard of colors having meaning except for determining your color profile—you know, so that you're wearing colors that complement your skin tones." Realizing that she was babbling out of nervousness, she said, "That's a pretty color you're wearing—is that mauve, or is it plum or burgundy?"

"All of the above. All of those shades, along with lavender, are considered purple—one of my favorite colors, because it's a balance between earth and sky, senses and spirit..." She stopped mid-sentence and asked, "Do you have a reservation with us today?"

"No," Jud said. "By the way, what is it that you do here—I mean exactly, Ms. Maude Carberry?" he asked, reading the name sign on the reception desk.

The woman laughed. "Oh, that's not me. Maude is out on...an extended leave." She snatched up the name plate and said, "I'm Rachel. And who are you? Do you have a reservation?"

"Judson...um...Davis," he said. "These are my nieces, Parker and Pamela."

Rachel acknowledged the women, and the detective continued, "No, we don't have a reservation. But we'd like to make one. What is it that you do here? What do you think my nieces would enjoy? The cost doesn't matter. We're actually touring the San Francisco area. We've grown tired of the city and the shopping and all. We came up to see about buying a winery and someone told us we might enjoy the experience you provide here." He looked around. "It certainly is a beautiful resort. Is it a resort? Is that how you would describe it, Miss Rachel?"

Rachel shook her head. "Not exactly. We provide a variety of dance classes and..." She looked at Olivia again and brightened. "We also offer a high tea experience that you might be interested in. Are you folks ready for tea?"

"With the cat?" Parker asked.

"Especially with the cat," Rachel said. "The high priestess would adore meeting her."

"You have a high priestess?" Pamela asked, wide-eyed.

"Yes."

"Of what?" Jud asked. When he saw the look on Rachel's face, he said, "I'm new to all this stuff my nieces are into. Can you catch me up to speed?"

"How about if I arrange for tea with High Priestess Seraphina?" Rachel suggested. "She can tell you what you need to know."

"Sure," Jud said, pulling an envelope and a pen from his pocket. He removed the parchment paper that had the emblem on it from the envelope and laid it in on the desk front of himself readying his pen. He asked, "How do you spell that? I want to write it down."

Rachel stared at the piece of paper and said, "Well, it appears, Mr. Davis, that you've already met Seraphina or one of her assistants."

Jud and Parker exchanged a glance and he asked, "Why would you say that?"

She pointed. "You're carrying a replica of her symbol."

"Yeah, I don't actually remember where I picked that up," he said.

"It's Seraphina's *crest*, you might say," Rachel explained.

"Well, then, yes," he agreed. "We definitely want to meet her."

"I'm sure High Priestess Seraphina will enjoy that," Rachel said. She smiled at Olivia as the cat rested in Parker's arms. "She'll especially take pleasure in meeting the allegorical cat." Before Parker could question the unusual phrase, Rachel pressed a button on a desk pad and said, "Victoria, please arrange for high tea. High Priestess Seraphina has guests." She looked up at the trio again and said, "It will be a few minutes, would you like to tour the gardens while you wait? Oh, by the way, the audience with the High Priestess is a hundred dollars each, payable in advance."

"And the dance classes?" Parker asked.

Rachel frowned. "You really want to dance? I didn't get that. I thought that was a ruse." When the others looked at her she said, "Oh, many of us here are second-sighted, you might say—you know, perceptive beyond the reality we're taught from birth."

"You're witches?" Pamela questioned.

Ignoring her, Rachel led the trio to a door and opened it to reveal a lovely arbor of roses and colorful gardens beyond. "Enjoy," she said. "I'll let you know when Effie—er…a…High Priestess Seraphina is ready."

"Effie," Parker hissed once Rachel had disappeared back into the lobby.

"I heard," Jud said. "It sounds like we've come to the right place. I just hope that high whatchamacallit gal knows where my daughter is." He gazed beyond the gardens into the distance. "I'd sure like to know what's on the other side of that wall."

"That's quite a wall," Pamela said.

"That it is," Jud muttered. "It's calling to me."

Parker chuckled. "Calling to you? Jud, I've never heard you speak of your sixth sense like that."

When Olivia pulled Parker off balance, Jud chuckled. "What's she after, a lizard? There are certainly plenty of plantings for reptiles to hide in."

"And cats," Pamela said, pointing.

Parker chuckled. "Oh, is that what you're interested in, Olivia? Do you want to play with those kitty-cats?"

"I don't think so," Jud said. He pointed. "She wants to go *that* way."

"I don't know about this," Parker said, hesitantly following Olivia. She suddenly stopped and hissed, "Do you guys hear that? It sounds like someone's chanting."

"Yeah, probably one of the wannabe witches doing a cleansing or something," Pamela said. "Come on, let's see where Olivia is taking us. There!" she whispered.

Parker stopped when she saw a woman sitting on a bench with her eyes closed. She turned away, muttering, "Well, she doesn't need us getting in her space." She reached for Olivia, then yelped when the frisky calico broke away from her. "Oh no," Parker said. "She wants to go bother that woman. Olivia!" she hissed when the determined cat sauntered closer to where the woman sat amidst a grotto of flowering shrubs. "I'm so sorry," Parker said, picking up Olivia. "I didn't mean to disturb you." She turned to leave.

"Wait!" the woman called. "Do you work here?"

"No," Parker said. "I thought maybe you did. No, we're just visiting. It's quite a place, isn't it?"

"I guess so, but I don't think it's a very safe place. They seem to have lost my mother."

"What?" Parker asked. "They lost her? Today? Did she come here today? Maybe she went out for a walk after the dance class, or she's having a cup of tea with the high priestess."

"The what?" the woman asked. She shook her head. "No, she didn't come here today. She came here several days ago." She looked at the others and continued, "Heaven knows why. Mom is always searching for something—a better understanding of life and death, a view into the other side. She constantly tries to communicate with my grandparents and especially my aunt, who are all dead, you know." She winced. "You caught me actually trying one of Mom's meditations in an attempt to reach her. I'm getting desperate here." She shifted on the bench in order to face the others. "Maybe you were sent to help me. Is that why you're here?"

Jud shrugged, then asked, "So what makes you think your mother is here?"

The woman gazed at him for a moment and explained, "Mom is a mystical or spiritual junkie, you might say. She was so excited to learn about this place. It took weeks for her to get an invitation. The day finally came, and she told us—my brother and me—where she was going and all, then she drove out here, and we haven't seen or heard from her since." She glanced toward the building and admitted, "I sneak onto the grounds a couple of times a day, walk around, and sit and wait hoping to see her. I wonder if they've hypnotized her and she can't wake up or she's in a stupor and doesn't know where she is. I've tried talking to that girl in the lobby, and I've caught a few of the scullery maids, but…"

"Scullery maids?" Pamela repeated.

The woman glanced at her and said, "Well, I sure don't know what else to call them. I see them around here wearing those odd flowing gowns, cloaks, and aprons—well, some of them wear aprons. They remind me of the scullery maids in the fairytales Mom used to read to me. Anyway, those people won't even look at me, let alone talk to me. Some of them seem rather dim—you know, dull, like they're drugged or under a spell." She looked up at the others and slumped. "No one I've talked to seems to know anything, and they won't let me talk to someone who does."

"Oh my gosh. I'm so sorry." Parker said.

When Olivia bumped up against the woman she jumped, then smiled and petted her. "Hi, kitty," she cooed. "Aren't you pretty? Is this your cat?" she asked. "I see cats peeking at me from under the shrubs, but those don't seem friendly." She cupped Olivia's face in her hands. "You're sure sweet. What's your name?"

"Olivia," Parker said, smiling at the interaction between Olivia and the distraught woman.

"Have you checked with the authorities?" Jud asked. "You might want to file a missing-person report."

With more energy, the woman said, "Yes. Yes, I did. Do you know what they told me? That I'm not the first one to issue such a complaint. They said their investigations all lead to the same thing—the individuals drove off the property in their cars, and they have cameras here to prove it." She leaned forward. "Do you know what the authorities' theory is? Mom and the other people—three or four of them, I think, were so inspired by what they learned here that they chose a new path in life or simply went on a retreat. The officer I spoke with explained that many of the clients or students are advised to go on a secret retreat to finish the work they started here—at least that's what a spokesperson from here told him."

"Do they have another facility somewhere else?" Jud asked.

The woman shook her head. "I don't know. I just can't get any information from anyone. I feel so alone and shut out. I guess it's all about protecting their clients' privacy."

"Their clients?" Jud repeated. He mumbled, "It's more like their victims."

Parker glanced at him, then suggested to the woman, "Maybe you could somehow get in touch with the others who are in the same quandary as you are."

The woman nodded. "I've thought about that, but I'm not sure how to get that sort of information." She smiled when Olivia jumped up next to her on the bench and lay against her. "What a sweet, sweet being," she said, caressing Olivia's fur. She then said, "I'm just so positive that whatever happened to Mom happened here. They did something to her or are doing something to her, and she's here someplace on this property." Before anyone else could speak, she added, "Oh, and she had just bought a new Jaguar, and it certainly isn't out there in the parking area. I think they took her car."

"Well, that could have happened anywhere," Jud said. "In the city, in a rural area, in the mountains..."

"I know that," the woman said, "but as I said, I sense her near when I'm here. You have to understand, Mom and I are very close."

Jud looked at the enormous wall again and asked, "Can you sense what's behind there? Do you think your mother's in that area?"

"No," she said. "No I don't, but I do believe something sinister is behind that wall. I've tried to penetrate it—you know, with my mind. So far I haven't succeeded. It's all just scrambled. My mind is scrambled when I try to penetrate that wall." She looked up at the trio. "What are you doing here? You aren't going to let them do something to you, are you? Which of you are going in there?"

"All of us," Pamela said, grinning.

Jud nodded. "Yeah, we're having high tea with the high magistrate or majesty or..."

"Priestess," Pamela said, grinning.

"You're going to meet her in person?" the woman asked, surprised. "They won't let me even make an appointment with her."

"Yeah, I can see why they wouldn't," Parker said. When the woman looked at her, she explained, "I mean, if they think your intentions aren't, you know, to their liking. You've accused them of harboring or harming your mother, right?"

The woman nodded.

"Where are you staying, Ms…" Jud started.

"Bledsoe. Felicia Bledsoe. Mom's name is Doris Schafer, in case you get any vibes that I've missed."

"Yeah, okay," he said, clearing his throat self-consciously. "So where are you staying?"

"I planned to drive back home to LA tonight, but I'm flexible. What do you have in mind?"

"I'm not sure," Jud said, rubbing his chin and gazing at the wall, "but I might want to talk to you some more. And I'd like to help you find your mother."

"Who are you?" the woman asked. "Do you have powers to counter those of whoever is in charge here?"

"Oh," he said, chuckling, "I don't know about that. I'd just like to meet the woman and see what bull she's selling. And I want to get a look behind that wall. Maybe we could use a drone."

"Yes," Felicia said, excitedly. "Then we will stay on at least for another few days. Want to take down my information?"

"We?" Jud questioned.

"My brother's with me." She grinned. "In fact, he's out purchasing a drone as we speak."

Jud nodded his approval, and took his phone from his pocket to record where Felicia and her brother were staying.

Parker beat him to it. "Give that information to me," she said, preparing her phone for the input. "Jud is all fumble-fingers when it comes to his phone." She added, "By the way, "I'm Parker, this is my cousin, Pamela, and this is Detective Jud Caldwell."

"Detective?" Felicia repeated.

He put his finger across his lips. "Shhh."

Just then they heard Rachel call, "Mr. Davis, party of three, plus the beautiful calico. Your table is ready."

Jud glanced at the others and said, "Well, let's go see what we can learn, shall we, girls?"

"Mr. Davis?" Felicia repeated quietly.

Jud winked at her. "Today, yes." When Parker caught up to the others with Olivia in her arms, he complained to her, "Fumble-fingers?"

She chuckled. "I've seen you try to put someone's number into your phone. It takes you forever."

"And we're in a hurry?" he asked.

"Yes, I don't want to miss high tea," she said.

He grinned at her, then looked at Olivia. "Has she had her spa day out here yet?"

"I certainly hope so," Parker said.

"Spa day?" Pamela questioned.

Parker leaned closer to her and said, "He means has she gone potty."

"Oh," Pamela said, looking at Olivia.

"You're not much of a cat person, are you?" Parker asked.

Pamela shook her head. "I never had the opportunity to connect with cats or any other kind of animal."

"You never had a pet?" Parker asked.

"You don't want to know about the short lives of pets in the households where I lived. One of the foster homes had hamsters or guinea pigs or some type of rodent." She shuddered. "We were always finding them dead in their cages and under furniture."

Parker winced.

"Follow me quietly," Rachel instructed when the trio caught up to her. She led the group across the spacious lobby, through a small hallway, past a flight of stairs, and into a darkened room on the ground floor, instructing, "Please be seated at the table." She pointed. "That's High Priestess Seraphina's place. Have a lovely tea," she added before quietly exiting the room.

Once Jud and Pamela had chosen their seats, Parker took Olivia's bed out of her tote and placed it on the floor next to a third chair. "Lie down in your little bed, love-love," she urged. She chuckled. "Oh, well, then just stretch out there on the floor."

Jud grinned. "She certainly can't stretch out in that tiny bed you brought for her."

"She does love to stretch," Parker said. "She can stretch practically double her length, but she also likes to fit herself into tiny places like this nice traveling bed." She rolled her eyes. "Unless I want her to, then she just lays on any old dirty floor." She shivered, then glanced around. "What was that?"

"What?" Jud asked.

"I felt a chill," Parker said.

"I felt it too," Pamela said, sounding a little breathless. She looked around. "That was eerie. Where did it come from?"

Parker shook her head. "Heck if I know."

"Probably an air vent," Jud reasoned.

"Hello," came a booming female voice from behind them. "I'm delighted that you've come to see me, especially Vivienne."

The others looked at each other, and Pamela mouthed, "Vivienne?"

The woman, dressed in a heavy brocade costume, stopped in the middle of the room and looked around. "Where is she? You brought her, didn't you?" When she saw that her guests were bewildered, the woman said, "Oh, I'm told that you know her as Olivia. Is she with you or not?" she barked.

"Olivia? Yes," Parker said, standing up to greet the woman, who appeared to be about seventy with silver curls framing her face and a headpiece embedded with what looked to be authentic gems. Her exquisitely embroidered gown was also decorated with jewels scattered across the bodice.

"Please sit down," the woman said, "I'll tell you when and if you need to rise. For now, sit."

The trio watched as the woman seemed to float to the empty chair, then fold herself into it. She picked up a bell and rang it. Immediately a young man appeared wearing slacks and a shirt in shades of purple, along with a wide black sash. He carried a tray with a teapot and four sets of teacups and saucers.

With a wave of her hand, the woman said, "I'll do the pouring. Thank you, Travis."

This caught Jud's ear, and he turned to look as the young man quickly left the room.

"Is something wrong, Mr. Davis?" she asked. "By the way, I'm High Priestess Seraphina."

"High priestess of what?" Jud asked. When the woman stopped in mid-pour and looked at him, he shrugged. "Well, I thought it was a fair question. Of a church or a cult or…"

"You obviously wouldn't understand," she spat, awkwardly spilling a little tea into a saucer. She soaked up the spill with a flowered napkin and handed the cup and saucer to Jud, who sat closest to her. "Please pass this along to Parker," she said. "Parker, where is the magnificent Vivienne?"

"Olivia," Parker corrected. "She's right here." She tilted her head and asked, "How do you know my name?"

Ignoring her, Seraphina poured another cup of tea, handed it to Jud, and said, "For Pamela." Once the tea was served, she took a sip and asked, "May I have a look at her? Just place her up here on the table. I want to see her."

"On the table?" Parker questioned.

"Yes," the woman said impatiently. "If I say it, I mean it. On the table. I want to see her." When Parker complied, Seraphina's face softened into a smile. "Oh yes, she is exquisite, just as Rachel said. Beautiful." She gazed into Olivia's eyes, and the cat stared back at her. "She is all-knowing. Did you know that, Parker, that she is all-knowing?"

"Oh, um…well, she can outsmart me sometimes."

Seraphina nodded. "I imagine she does, you poor naive being"

Parker and Pamela exchanged looks.

Seraphina gazed at Olivia for quite a few more moments, then she took a sip of tea and asked, "So Mr. Davis, you are looking to buy a winery north of here?"

"Yes," he said, "at least one."

"Wonderful." She asked the women. "How do you like the tea?"

"It's delightful," Parker said.

Pamela nodded.

"So, Rachel tells me you ladies came for the dance. Are you into mysticism? You know the brand of dance we offer here is rather hypnotic and even sometimes hallucinatory," Seraphina explained.

"Do you serve spirits or supply home-grown tobacco to your students?" Jud asked.

Seraphina glared at him, then she began to laugh, finally saying, "No, Mr. Davis. It's the music and the movement that creates the arena, or the atmosphere, if you will, for the mesmerizing effects that many of our students experience. For some it's simply a gentle spirituality. Others have rather dark encounters within. It's whatever you want it to be, and sometimes something unexpected will stir within you." She leaned closer to Jud. "Most often students do not even have an inkling of what their experience will be. It depends on what you were born with and what has been instilled in you. Each being's experience is unique—not something we can predict. Will you women have a lovely experience in our dance studio or one that is troubling? I do not know, but I do know that you have something I want." She bore her eyes into Parker's and ran her hand over Olivia's fur.

"What?" Parker asked. "Oh wait, Olivia? No. She's not for sale, and I have no interest in re-homing her. No."

"I'm sorry dear lady, the covenant is made. The higher power has spoken." Seraphina's voice seemed to drop an octave as she practically growled, "Olivia will stay with me." Before Parker could respond, she added, "But she is no longer Olivia. She is Vivienne."

Parker stood up and reached for Olivia just as Travis returned to the room in a hurry with another young man dressed exactly like him. Seraphina clutched Olivia and forced her toward Travis.

"No!" Parker said. She rushed forward, but felt someone restrain her. "No!" she screamed, fighting to break loose.

At that, Jud stepped in. He ran after Travis, but was stopped by two more young men. One of them swung what appeared to be a lead pipe and hit him across the midriff, and two men carried Jud by the arms back into the room. He yanked away from them and started to make another move when he saw all three of the men blocking the entrance to where they had taken Olivia. He glared at them, then at Seraphina, snarling, "That was a cheap shot."

Ignoring him, the high priestess attempted to console Parker. "Now dear, you can get another cat.

There are hundreds of thousands of homeless cats. Why, perhaps you saw cats on the property. Take one. Take any that you see. They have no merit as far as I'm concerned, except as pets to keep my favorite lady-in-waiting content."

"You won't get away with this," Parker spat. "Olivia belongs with me."

"No, no, dear," the woman said calmly. "She's destined to be my cat—to work with me. That's why you found your way here today with her. The powers above us and those below us led you here to bring me Vivienne." She stood up, bowed slightly to Parker, and walked past her out of sight.

"No!" Parker screamed.

Jud watched the woman disappear into the next room, then he gazed at the young men who still stood guard. He took Parker's arm. "Come on, let's go. It won't do us any good to fight her on her turf." He whispered in Parker's ear, "We'll get her back."

Parker jerked away from him and spat, "Like you got your daughter back?"

Stunned at her retort, Jud quickly led Parker out of the room and back toward the lobby. When they reached the lobby Jud looked around and realized that Pamela was not with them. He looked into the hallway, then took a few steps in that direction, but was stopped when a door slid across the opening. "Pamela," he said. "Parker, your cousin didn't come out with us."

Parker gasped. "Oh my gosh." She trotted to where the receptionist worked at her desk. "Rachel," she called, "that woman took Olivia, and Pamela is still in there. Can you open that door? We have to go find them."

There was no response.

"Rachel," Parker said more loudly, "we need help."

"I'm sorry," the receptionist said, continuing to focus on her work.

Jud took Parker's arm and ushered her out through the front door. Once outside, she pulled away. "Jud, what do you think you're doing? We have to go get Pamela and Olivia."

"And get ourselves and them maybe killed?" he growled.

Parker went limp. "Oh my gosh. Jud, what do you think goes on in there? What are they going to do to Olivia and poor Pamela? It can't be anything good." She buried her face in her hands, then she began to prattle, "People go in there and they disappear. You heard Felicia." She grabbed his arm and pulled him toward the car. "Come on, let's go get the police."

"No police," Jud said, walking with her to the car.

"No police?" Parker screeched. "What do you mean? Jud, Pamela and Olivia could be in serious danger. How in the world did they get her, anyway? Did you see them grab Pamela?"

Jud shook his head and said more quietly, "I got the impression that she stayed behind on purpose."

"What?" Parker shouted. "Oh, Jud, I'm so worried.

"We'll get her back," he said, "both of them."

"When that witch finds out how naughty Olivia can be, she might give her away or worse," Parker complained. She scowled. "I do not trust that woman. There's something terribly wrong with her."

"I know, Parker," Jud said quietly. "It'll be okay. I can almost guarantee it."

She faced him with daggers in her eyes. "Almost guarantee it? What in the heck does that mean?"

"Get in the car and buckle up," he said. "Let's see if we can find Felicia. I want to meet with her and her brother. With more of us involved, we might have a better chance of having all the missing people and the cat returned to us."

Parker could not keep her eyes off the Dunbar compound. Jud had just shifted into gear when she shouted, "Wait! Jud, wait, there's Pamela." She fumbled to release her seat belt, then leaped from the car and ran to her, calling, "Pamela, what happened?"

"Let's get out of here," Pamela hissed, grabbing Parker and pulling her toward the car. "Get in, and I'll tell you about it."

Parker ran along with Pamela to the car and quickly got into the front seat. Pamela hurled herself into the back.

When Jud heard both doors close he drove off. "Are we being chased?" he asked, glancing in his rearview mirror. When he saw no one, he asked, "What's the hurry? What happened to you, anyway, Pamela? Where were you? I thought you were behind us when we left the queen's chambers."

Pamela chuckled nervously and corrected him. "The high priestess." She buckled her seat belt and let out a long breath. "Wow! That was weird as all get-out. I've gotten myself into a lot of situations, but nothing quite like that one."

"What happened?" Parker asked, turning in her seat. "Did you see where they took Olivia? Is she okay?"

"Yeah, she's okay," Pamela said. "I saw her sitting on a satin pillow inside a foo-foo cage. She looks fine."

"You saw where they took her?" Parker squealed. "How did you get in there? You're sure she's okay? They aren't going to use her in some sort of sacrificial ritual, are they?"

Pamela shook her head. "I don't know what they have planned—whether they'll worship her or what—but she's being pampered now."

"Did you see the lock on the pen?" Parker asked. "What kind of latch is on there?"

Pamela looked confused. "Huh?"

"Olivia is an escape artist when it comes to simple latches, and I've seen her manage some more intricate locks, too." She shook her head. "Darn, I can't decide if I'd rather she escape or if she'd be better off staying put." She winced. "Oh, I'm just so worried about her." She looked back at Pamela. "And they'd better not be spoiling her so she's bratty when I get her back."

Jud chuckled. "You hope *they* don't spoil her? How much more spoiled could that cat be?" He glanced at Pamela in the rearview mirror, "So, what happened in there? Did they grab you, or did you lag behind and stay for some reason?"

"Yeah, I held back a little hoping to learn something—you know, about what they're going to do with the cat and us and maybe Felicia's mom. I thought I could either ask questions or snoop."

"Oh my gosh, Pamela, that was courageous. What made you…? I didn't know you were…" Parker started.

"I've tried to tell you, I've had my share of exploits," Pamela said, "even in the world of witchcraft and all that stuff."

"Witchcraft?" Parker repeated.

"Yeah," Pamela cranked. "Parker, wake up; what do you think the encounter with that so-called high priestess was about? That wasn't any baby shower. The woman's dabbling in some weird stuff that could hurt people, and I'm pretty sure she doesn't know what she's doing. She could be dangerous, and I say that mostly because she seems a little crazy."

"Do ya think?" Jud said sarcastically.

"Hey, not everyone who enters the world of spells and curses and hexes is loopy, but those who are may be the most dangerous." Pamela continued, "Yeah, so when you left, the others retreated into that hallway without noticing me. I spent some time in the altar room…"

"Altar room?" Jud questioned.

"Where we had high tea. That would be considered a witch's altar room," Pamela explained. "I could tell by the way it's decorated. I doubt that she does the typical spells and sacrifices, because she's clearly a wannabe witch, but it's something she's evidently studied for a while, and she's having fun acting it out."

"But you think she could be dangerous?" Parker asked.

"Undoubtedly," Pamela said.

"And you say they're treating Olivia okay?" Parker asked. "You saw her sitting on a satin pillow? Where was that? Did you actually sneak around the place? Do you think we could break in and get her?"

Pamela laughed. "Well, I did sneak around a bit. The wannabe witch and her young men and a few of the scullery maids had their backs to me. They were all ooohing and aaahing over the cat. I eavesdropped for a few minutes, then turned to leave. One of the girls saw me. She ratted me out, and the chase was on."

"Pamela," Parker screeched, "it sounds like you enjoyed that."

"I sure did," Pamela said excitedly. "I felt alive. Yes, that was awesome." She sat with her thoughts for a moment, then continued, "So I ran to where I knew the door was, but it was locked. Yeah, locked from the outside, I guess. There may have been a secret latch somewhere, but I didn't have time to look for it. I saw a stained glass window— one of those with vertical panels that open and close. I looked at that thing, then looked back at the ghoulish mob chasing me, and I decided to go for it. I broke out part of the window with a big metal cross I found hanging on the wall, then I swung that thing around at the ghouls. I was pretty sure I could outrun them—I was a sprinter in high school, you know—so I made a break for it and luckily saw you just about to leave." She blew out a breath, saying, "And here I am."

"Gads," Parker said. "So you know where Olivia is. Jud, let's go back and get her."

The detective frowned at Parker. "I think we need to be cautious and work smart. We know of at least one person who's possibly being held on that property. We can't jeopardize a life by doing something stupid to rescue a cat. Besides, Pamela told you that she's being pampered. She's okay."

"Yeah," Pamela said, "until they decide they don't need her anymore."

"What?" Parker yelped, weakly.

"Well, it's possible that they plan to get what they can from the cat—you know, some sects consider cats sacred," Pamela explained. "They'll put her on a pedestal, glean what energy they can from her, then either discard or sacrifice her."

"No," Parker wailed.

Pamela leaned forward and said, "Jud, I'm not kidding. If that woman believes Olivia has enough spirit energy in her—if she is as special as they imagine she is—they just might offer her to their leader, imaginary or not. So I'd say we need to act quickly if we want to rescue Olivia."

"Oh my gosh, no," Parker said. "I should never have been so stupidly curious. I've endangered Olivia's life. Jud, you heard Pamela. We have to go back and get her."

"How, Parker?" he asked.

"Yeah, how?" Pamela said. "What I didn't tell you is there are dogs. Not only are there armed ghouls, there are dogs. I found out that the pretty window I broke looks out into a dog enclosure. The dogs were evidently locked in a wire run. I didn't see them until they were released. I got over the wall just before the dogs got to me."

"Good God," Jud said. "Are you talking about that twelve-foot wall? Is that where the dogs are? How did you manage to get over that?"

"Well, I also pole-vaulted in high school, but no, I didn't vault over *that* wall."

"You pole-vaulted?" Parker looked Pamela in the eyes and asked more quietly, "Are you making this up? It sounds like fiction to me."

Pamela laughed. "No." She pulled up her pants leg to reveal a scuffed knee. "Does this look like fiction? She shook her head. "I found an old rake they probably use to clean up the dog poop, and I vaulted myself over the wall." She rubbed her knee and said, "I guess I'm kind of out of practice."

"My gosh, Mellie," Parker said. "I had no idea…"

"I told you I've been around." She grinned and repeated, "Mellie. I haven't heard you call me that since we were kids living together in your mom's home." She patted her cousin's shoulder from the backseat. "Thanks, Par-Par, it means a lot."

Still reeling from Pamela's story, Parker simply stared ahead, her heart aching for Olivia.

## Chapter Six

"Felicia and her brother are meeting us here at the restaurant," Jud announced as he pulled into the café parking lot.

"Good," Pamela said. "I'm starving."

Parker nodded. "It seems like a long time ago that we ate your delicious breakfast casserole." She moaned. "I started to grab for Olivia before getting out. Darn, darn," she complained. "I should never have let her…"

"Parker," Pamela said, "you had no choice. We will get her back." She patted Jud on the shoulder as they both prepared to step out of the car. "Uncle Jud will make sure of that, right, Uncie?"

"I hope like hell you're right," he huffed.

The trio had been waiting at a table for just a few minutes when Parker pointed. "Here they come." She waved a hand to get their attention.

Once the newcomers had taken a seat Felicia introduced her brother, Raif, to the other, then glanced around and asked, "Where's your beautiful cat?" She told her brother, "Olivia is Parker's cat—a calico." When Parker slumped in her chair, Felicia gasped. "Did something happen?

"Let's order," Jud suggested, "then we'll catch you up to speed."

"So what happened?" Raif asked, handing his menu to the waitress.

"Did something happen to Olivia?" Felicia asked, concerned.

"That lowlife wannabe priestess has her," Pamela complained. "She invited us for tea all nice and friendly-like, then she stole Olivia."

Felicia put her hand on Parker's arm and said, "I'm so sorry.

"Thank you," Parker muttered. "I'm just worried sick. Pamela risked her life trying to get her back."

Felicia and Raif looked at Pamela, who said, "Yeah, but that witch sicced her warlocks and her dogs on me."

"They have dogs?" Felicia asked.

"Yes, mean ones," Pamela said, "with teeth."

Parker chuckled. "She had to break a window to get out."

"And pole-vault," Jud added.

"Pole-vault?" Raif asked, looking at Pamela.

Pamela nodded. "With a rake. As I told Jud and Parker, I'm more than a little out of practice since high school, but I managed to get over that wall before the dogs caught up to me."

"That monstrous wall?" Raif blurted.

Pamela shook her head. "No. This wall's only about five feet high. It's a smaller enclosure where they keep the dogs."

Jud leaned forward and spoke more quietly. "Raif, Felicia tells me you have a drone."

"Yes, but not with me, so I bought a new one this afternoon." When Jud winced, Raif explained, "I've been wanting to upgrade, anyway. This was a good excuse."

"What do you use them for?" Jud asked.

"I'm a filmmaker in Hollywood," Raif said. "The drone adds dimensions to filming that we might be able to accomplish, but that were awkward and sometimes downright dangerous before."

"I can imagine." Jud said. "So you know how to fly those things?"

Raif nodded. He asked, "What do you have in mind, Jud?"

"I'd like to see what's behind that gnarly wall. I mean, who would build a wall like that unless they have something mighty important to hide—something illegal, perhaps?"

"Gotcha," Raif quipped. "Yeah, I also wonder what that wall is hiding."

"So you've been to the place?" Jud asked.

"Yes, with Felicia yesterday."

Jud lowered his voice again. "It sounds like you believe as Felicia does that your mother has been detained. You don't think she just took an extended tour to wine country or something? Is

176

she married? Maybe she met someone and she's off seeing the big city with him."

Raif shook his head. "It's just too unusual for our mother to disappear—you know, go off on her own without letting us know. She even told us she was coming up to experience this place. No, she doesn't try to hide things. She's always been up-front with us, right, Felicia?"

His sister nodded. "Yes, even when she knows we're going to try talking her out of some of the things she wants to do."

"Did you try to talk her out of coming up here?" Parker asked.

"No," Felicia said. "We've learned it does no good. Mom is going to do what she wants to do, and we definitely don't want to discourage her from experiencing life her way. If we become the Gestapo, we're liable to be left in the dark about where she is and unable to track her down if she gets into trouble."

"Has she been in trouble before?" Jud asked.

"Oh yes," Felicia said, glancing at her brother. "We've had to bail her out a few times."

When the others looked surprised, Raif chuckled. "Not out of jail or anything, but she's kind of gullible and…"

"Yeah," Felicia said, "she once took a canoe ride in Brazil with a local who didn't speak English, and she ended up stranded in a town unable to communicate with anyone. Raif speaks Spanish, and he got on the phone with a merchant there and was able to get her back to the city before her flight left without her."

Raif chuckled and reminded his sister, "And there was the time you went to that health spa with Mom."

"Yes," Felicia said. "We each signed up for a massage that day, and we were supposed to meet afterward for a meditation class. Well, I waited and waited for Mom to show up. Finally I asked an employee and she said, 'Your mama went to the snake den.' Well, Mom is terrified of snakes, and I couldn't for the life of me figure out why she would sign up for that experience—it was a class on overcoming fears of things like snakes. Well, it turns out she thought it was a mythology class. They didn't use the term *snake*, they called it the 'serpent encounter.'"

"Yikes," Pamela said, "what did she do? I'd probably pee my…" She glanced around the table and clammed up.

Raif cleared his throat and asked, "So, Jud, what do you have in mind for tonight?"

Jud thought for a moment and said, "I'd like to use the drone, and see if we can figure out what goes on behind that wall. It's a large enough area in there and seemingly secure. They could be building bombs or running a human trafficking operation or…" He shook his head. "It's just hard to imagine, and I'd like to know before we make our move."

"What do you envision our move being?" Felicia asked.

Jud shrugged. "We can figure that out once we know more about their operation." He faced Parker. "I've been thinking…"

"Uh-oh," she muttered. "Do I want to hear this?"

He grinned at her, then said, "I think we need someone on the inside."

"What?" Parker yelped. "I'm not going in there with dogs and ghouls and …"

"This may not actually require going inside ourselves," Jud assured her. "What I'd like to do is have you girls befriend one of the slaves."

"Slaves?" Parker repeated.

"You know what I mean—those girls or women who ride the bikes around wearing those cloaks. I caught a glimpse of one or two of them in the gardens while we were waiting to have that fancy tea party. We need to find someone who will do a reveal—you know, spill some of the fake queen's beans. I'd especially like to know if my daughter's among them."

"Your daughter?" Felicia asked, surprised. "You're daughter's one of them?"

Jud shrugged. "I don't know. She's missing, and our investigation has led us here. Since those female slaves hide their identity in all of that fabric they wear, I have to wonder…"

"And veils," Parker added. "Those that threatened me in the ladies room at the park wore veils."

"I know one of them," Felicia said quietly. When the others looked at her, she explained, "Her name is Karma. She's a sweet thing. She sat with me out back there for a while yesterday afternoon." She winced. "I got the impression that she hasn't been there for long and that she really doesn't want to be there, but she's somehow unable to leave."

This sparked Jud's interest. "I was pretty sure of that." He leaned in. "I mean, that some of them are being held against their will by some unknown force or threat or..." He took a ragged breath and said for Felicia's and Raif's benefit, "I believe that if my daughter's there, it's because she's under some sort of duress, but what? That's what I don't know." He looked at Felicia, then Raif. "I wonder if it's the same for your mother. Are they holding her against her will for some sinister reason?"

The siblings glanced at each other and Raif said, "I can't imagine why. I keep going over possible reasons in my mind, and I can't for the life of me figure out what someone like this supposed high priestess would want with our mother."

More quietly, Jud said, "Felicia indicates that your mother has money, that she drove a new Jag up here to visit the phony queen. But it's not in the parking lot, is it?"

Raif sat up straighter and huffed, "No! Oh dear, God. Do you think that's it? They took her car and they're trying to get her to sign over her bank accounts or something?"

"Spiritual organizations have been doing that for years," Jud said.

Felicia frowned. "Oh my gosh, you're right. We see it happening in churches—even those thought to be on the up and up. People are guilted into giving away their property and money. It appears that Madam Seraphina is going a step above or below if she's actually kidnapping her followers and holding them captive or worse."

"Mom might not be on the property at all," Raif said. "They could have taken her to another location, which would make it even more difficult or even impossible to find her." He looked at Jud. "I like your idea of trying to talk to one of the…um… slaves."

Felicia took a deep breath. "Yes, if we go back to that place, I'll see if I can find Karma. She was one of two girls I saw caring for the cats. There are a lot of cats on the property." She smiled. "The other girl wears the cutest pink shoes. She's the only one I've seen there wearing something other than black or grey shoes."

Parker put her hand on Felicia's arm. "Can you ask Karma about Olivia? If we could find out where they're keeping her or if they've turned her loose or something, then maybe we can go in and get her."

"First things first," Jud said. When he had everyone's attention, he explained, "This could be an intricate operation. We need information before we barge in to do any rescuing of cats or people. First, I'd say we need to know if people are being held on that property against their will. And we need to know what's behind that wall. We'll use the drone to see what we can see. At the same time, Felicia, yes, I want you to find Karma. Parker, you go with Felicia. You'll know the type of questions to ask the girl. I want you to go gentle, you two. We don't want to spook her. I get that those young women are easily spooked, and I'd like to know what they're afraid of—what keeps them there and what they're afraid of, which may be the same thing."

"What do you want me to do, captain?" Pamela asked.

"You can come with Raif and me. We may need a woman's approach if we're discovered. You seem to be fairly quick on your feet. I think we can use your expertise."

"Wow!" Pamela said. "I have expertise?"

Parker nudged her and smiled. "Way to go, cuz." She edged her phone out of her pocket and looked at the screen. "It's Mom," she announced, walking out of the restaurant so as not to disturb anyone. "Hi, Mom!" she said. "How are you?"

"That's what I called to ask you," Elaine Campbell replied. "I haven't heard from you in a while."

"Yeah, it has been a few weeks, hasn't it?" Parker said. "I've been busy. Hey, Mom, guess who's living with me this week."

"Your cousin?" Elaine asked.

"Yes," Parker said. "How did you know?"

"It's just an educated guess. Before she left here she asked a lot of questions about you and the work you do and where you are now… I promise I did not give her the address to the condo you're staying in, but I figured if she wanted it, she'd find it somehow."

"She did," Parker said.

Elaine apologized. "I'm sorry, Par-Par."

"No problem, Mom. She's been a big help to our investigation." When Elaine remained silent, Parker said, "Mom, are you there?"

"Yes," Elaine said. "So she's not driving you crazy or getting in your way and all?"

"On the contrary," Parker said. "She may have found her niche, actually, she's been somewhat of a help."

"Well, all she was around here was annoying," Elaine said. "Don't you tell her I said that. It's just that…"

"I know exactly what you're saying, Mom. Some people have a personality that grates on your nerves. In fact, I was not a happy camper when she showed up. And she pulled some shenanigans when Houston was here that really made me furious, but today she's showing another side. The way things are going, she might just be my favorite cousin of all time."

"What's going on, Parker?" Elaine asked tentatively.

"Well, Mom," Parker said, her voice lowered, "Olivia is being held by a witch or a witch wannabe, as Mellie calls her, on a large exotic compound here outside of San Francisco, and my friend Jud's daughter is still missing after seven years. We think she might be on the compound as well. It turns out that Mellie knows something about fake witches and witchcraft and things."

"Why doesn't that surprise me?" Elaine asked.

Parker continued, "And she has taken some risks that may prove to be most valuable. Yes, I'm glad she came knocking on my door." Parker spoke even more quietly. "However, once everyone is back where they belong—Olivia, Jud's daughter, and others, and when I'm ready to go on to my next assignment, then what?"

"I was thinking the same thing," Elaine said.

Parker laughed. "Well, I'm going to strongly suggest that Pamela enroll in the police academy or maybe the military."

"Parker," Elaine shouted, "that's brilliant! A bit odd—I mean, I can't imagine Pamela in that role, but you think either of those possibilities would be a good match for her?"

"Absolutely. She seems to love the action and intrigue of investigative work. She isn't afraid to take chances. And she could use lessons in discipline and boundaries." Parker glanced toward the café and said, "Hey, Mom, we're discussing important strategy over lunch—or I guess you'd call it linner, it's too late to be lunch. I'd better get back. Thank you for calling. It's always good to talk to you."

"Oh yes," Elaine said. "Well, honey, you be careful. God, I hope you get sweet Olivia back. That's worrisome. I know how much you love her and she loves you."

"Thanks, Mom."

"Be careful, would you?"

"Sure will. Love you, Mom."

Late that afternoon, Jud parked his car a distance away from the Dunbar compound to let Parker and Felicia out. "Stay sharp," he said. "I'll wait here for you."

"If we don't come back?" Parker questioned.

"I'll get backup; don't you worry."

Parker rolled her eyes. "What sort of backup can you possibly find to counter that woman's spells?"

"She's a phony Parker," Pamela insisted. "Just watch out for the dogs. They're real."

"Thanks," Parker said with sarcasm. "That's comforting." She looked at Felicia. "Well, let's go see if we can find Karma, shall we?" Once the two women were on the compound grounds, Parker asked, "Where did you see Karma yesterday?"

"It was the day before," Felicia said. "I'd found my way to a bench somewhere in that large planting of shrubs, and she came along with a basket. She'd been picking herbs. There were cats with her—walking with her—but they scattered when they saw me."

"Let's start there. Show me where you were sitting."

"Okay," Felicia said, glancing around. "Come on."

As the two women made their way along narrow pathways among the foliage, Parker said, "Gosh, these little trails are everywhere."

Felicia nodded. "They have a lot of herbs growing out here. I imagine they pick daily to gather the things they need for the potions and brews."

"Potions and brews?" Parker repeated.

"You've heard of witches' brew. They use them for spells and ceremonies, and…" she hesitated.

"And what?" Parker asked.

"Well, I can't help but think Karma may have been under the influence of something—maybe a strong herb or a mixture of herbs."

"I noticed that bicyclist gal seemed subdued, too," Parker said. "I think we told you about the cyclist we thought rode off with Olivia earlier this morning." She glanced at Felicia as the two of them walked. "Do you know herbs? Do you see something growing here that could cause a sort of stupor if it were ingested?" She thought for a moment, then said, "Although, Rachel, the receptionist, didn't seem to be affected."

"No, but the people I saw in the gardens most certainly were," Felicia said, "or they are just bored with the work. Bored, burned out, whatever." Suddenly she put her hand out to stop Parker. "Listen," she whispered.

Parker nodded to their left, and they walked slowly toward the sound of someone mournfully singing. As they drew near, they could see a figure through the cover of shrubbery.

"Karma?" Felicia called quietly.

The young woman asked, "Who is it? Lucy?"

"It's me, Felicia." She pushed through the bushes and said, "Karma, I'd like to talk to you. May we talk again?"

Karma glanced toward the building, which was barely visible through the overgrowth.

"Oh, you have cats with you. Look how pretty they are," Felicia crooned. "Karma, this is my friend, Parker. May we sit with you and the cats?"

Karma glanced briefly at Parker and nodded. "This is Zelena," she said, petting a large fluffy grey cat in her lap. "That's Locasta over there, and the striped boy is Gandalf."

"Witches and Warlocks," Felicia muttered.

Karma nodded and continued petting the grey cat.

"How many cats do you have here," Parker asked gently, kneeling down and petting a mostly white cat.

"I don't know," Karma said. "I've never counted them. I just know who they are so I know if any of them is missing." She looked curiously at the women. "Why are you here? There are no appointments with Effie…Seraphina, after four. It's after four, isn't it?"

Felicia nodded. "We just want to visit with you. That's why we came back. I so enjoyed our visit before. I wanted to see you again."

"You did?" Karma asked.

"Yes," Felicia said. "And I wanted my friend to meet you."

Karma glanced at Parker again, expressionless.

"How long have you been here, Karma?" Parker asked.

"Here?" she repeated. "Almost four years. They brought me here when they opened. Some of the girls were before I came. They found Lucy a long time ago and Veronica. They get to go out sometimes to bring back store-bought and bartered things for the kitchen and the ceremonies." She brightened just a little. "Lucy and Veronica almost brought us a new cat this morning, but the cat got out of Veronica's basket. The cat came here anyway. Effie willed the cat to come, and she is here now. That is a reason to celebrate, so I'm picking herbs for a special celebration tea for this evening." She stood up. "I'd better get back with my basket. Effie doesn't like it when I shilly-shally."

"Shilly-shally," Parker repeated, chuckling.

Karma looked at her unsmiling, then turned to leave.

"Karma," Felicia said, "please, can I ask you one more thing?"

Karma stopped, and Felicia smiled sweetly. "Do the people who come here get to stay over? I mean, is there a room or a place where guests sometimes stay?"

The young woman stared into Felicia's face and nodded. "Yes," she said sounding mechanical, "Effie provides nice living quarters for those who want extra time with her—extra knowledge." She shook her head. "Sometimes they don't know they need extra work, but Effie knows and she provides it."

"How long do they stay?" Felicia asked.

"As long as is necessary," Karma said. "Sometimes they stay—they can't be trusted to leave." She looked at the women and started to bolt, when Parker stepped closer.

"What about you, Karma," Parker asked, "and Veronica and Lucy? What makes you stay? Do you want to stay or are you being made to stay?"

"We can leave," Karma said weakly, "but it is in our best interest to stay. Effie knows what's best for us." She turned away, saying, "I must go now."

"Wow!" Parker said. "That was a quick exit."

"Wasn't it?" Felicia agreed. "Like she vanished." She looked at Parker. "So what did we learn?"

Parker thought for a moment. "That those girls are probably being drugged—maybe with overdoses of some of the herbs Karma picks. They're probably also being brainwashed."

Felicia added, "And it sounds like that charlatan is holding people against their will."

"People and Olivia," Parker said. "But where and why?"

"Raif's drone may give some clarity on those questions," Felicia said. She glanced around. "Shall we try to find our way out of this maze and report to the detective?"

"Let's do," Parker said, taking a few steps, then she stopped and yelped, "Olivia?"

"What?" Felicia asked. "Your cat? Is that your cat?"

Parker let out a deep sigh. "I guess not. When I saw the coloring I thought for a moment…" She kneeled down and petted a large calico cat. "Hi there. What are you doing out here? I thought that woman worshipped cats like you. Does she know you're here?"

"What did she tell you?" Felicia asked, chuckling. "Did she answer your questions?"

Parker shook her head. "No." She pointed. "Look, there's another calico—oh, and another one. There are calicos all over the place. Why did she have to take Olivia?"

"Because she could," Felicia said. "That woman seems to have no boundaries, and she's power hungry. Oh, she just makes me so mad," she spat.

"Yeah, who does she think she is?" Parker griped. She ran her hand over the large calico again and acknowledged the other cats. "Take care, kitty-cats. Be safe. Maybe we can rescue you all. I know a great place where you can live out your life with kind ladies who will love you for you, not for what you can do for them."

"You do?" Felicia asked, as the two women wound their way out of the maze of pathways through dense vegetation.

"Yes," Parker said, "and it's not far from here. A group of women operate a beautiful cat colony—one of the oldest in the area and maybe the world."

"Nice," Felicia said.

The women had made their way along narrow pathways amidst shrubbery and vines for a few minutes when they both stopped, startled. "Hello," Parker said when she came face to face with another young woman, who was holding a black cat. She stared into the woman's face, then said, "Hannah?"

The young woman stared at her through large eyes, then lowered the cat to the ground, turned, and darted out of sight.

"Hannah!" Parker called.

"Hannah?" Felicia questioned.

Parker stared after the young woman and muttered, "I'm pretty sure that was Jud's daughter, the one they call Lucy. Dang, if only…" she started. She then said, "Well, at least we know she's here and not living someplace where she'll never be found. That's the good news. Yes, I'm almost positive that was Hannah, from the pictures I've seen." She pointed. "Come on, let's go in the direction she went. Maybe we'll find our way out of here."

It wasn't long before the women approached Jud's car. Raif leaped out of the front passenger seat and opened the back door for the women, who climbed in quickly.

"Whoa!" Parker yelped when Jud pulled away from the curb a little faster than she expected. "Why are you so eager to split out of there? Were we being watched or something?"

"You never know," Jud said. "In situations like this, you don't want to let any grass grow under your feet." He asked, "How did it go? What did you find out?"

"Quite a bit, actually," Parker said.

"Well?" he spat impatiently. "Out with it."

"It seems that Effie—that's the witch…"

"So it was established that she's a witch?" Jud asked.

"Wouldn't you say that's what she is or is trying to be?" Parker countered.

"Go on," Jud said, ignoring her question.

Parker grinned at him and continued. "We talked to Karma and she said Effie—you know, Seraphina—does *invite* people to stay over sometimes when she thinks they need to receive more instruction or information than they can get in one session, and there is a place on the grounds where they stay."

"Obviously, against their will," Felicia added.

"What makes you say that?" Jud asked.

Felicia explained, "Like I said, if Mom was able to, she'd let us know where she is. If she's still there, it is not because she has consented." She thought for a moment and said, "Well, I just can't imagine she'd consent to staying anyplace where she's not allowed to place a call to us, right, Raif?"

Before he could respond, Parker blurted, "Jud, we found some really pretty calico cats out in the yard. I think they had been discarded."

"Discarded?" he asked.

Parker nodded. "My guess is that once the creepy witch is finished with her spells or her ceremonies with the calico of the day, she turns them loose to fend for themselves. The girls—you know, Karma and the others—take care of them, but I'm not sure that's because Effie wants them to. Oh, and we think we met Hannah."

Jud remained silent. It appeared he was having trouble holding it together, then he asked, his voice strained. "Tell me, damnit! Tell me."

"She was with the cats," Parker said quietly. "We were trying to find our way out of the maze of herb bushes when we almost bumped into her. She was as startled as we were—maybe more so. I called her by name, and she ran off." Parker glanced at Felicia. "We think those girls are being drugged."

"I still believe it's a spell," Pamela insisted. When Felicia looked curiously at Pamela she explained, "Anyone can use hypnosis. Along with an herb cocktail and maybe even drugs, the right hypnosis technique can dull an otherwise bright and aware mind."

"So she *is* there?" Jud muttered.

"I'm pretty sure she is," Parker said.

"Oh, God, this is getting real. Are you telling me she's just an arm's-length away?"

"I think so," Parker confirmed.

Jud let out a long breath. "Well, let's go to Raif's and Felicia's place and get some rest, shall we? We have a big night ahead of us."

It was nearly midnight when Jud nudged Parker awake. "Let's go," he said.

"Huh?" she murmured sitting up. She stretched. "Oh, I must have fallen asleep here on the sofa. That was nice," she said, yawning. When she realized that Felicia and Raif were in the room, she said, "Thank you for letting us crash here with you."

"Yeah, this is a pretty nice pad," Pamela said, slipping into her shoes.

"Felicia explained, "We didn't know how long we'd be here,  so Raif and I talked the owner of this little house into renting it to us for a month. We told him we'd pay a month's rent no matter how long we needed it. He was happy, and we've sure found it to be comfortable and convenient." She smiled at Parker. "I'm glad you all got some sleep. It was a rough day."

"For all of us," Parker said quietly. She asked, "So do we have a plan?"

"Right to the point, huh?" Raif quipped.

"As she should be," Jud said. He handed Parker a set of keys. "You drive. We'll show you where to stop."

After a short time Jud instructed Parker to pull over to the curb. "You and Felicia go on—just drive around or go back to the house and wait if you want. We'll operate the drone from a distance. We don't want to set off any alarms or cameras on the property."

"Okay," Parker said. "Be careful." When she saw Pamela climb out of the car, she asked, "You're going with them?"

"Yes," Jud said. "We may need her. If you don't hear from us by one forty-five, call the cops. Tell them what you know so far."

"Oh no," Parker complained. "Would Olivia survive a raid? That woman might…"

Jud simply turned and walked away down the street with Raif and Pamela.

"Gads," Parker said, "it was kind of unnerving being on that property earlier, but I think *not* being part of Jud's surveillance team is going to be worse."

"I know what you mean," Felicia said.

"So what do you want to do?" Parker asked.

"Get a cup of hot coffee?" Felicia suggested.

196

"In this small village?" Parker asked. "Is there any place open this time of night?"

"There's an all-night gas station," Felicia said.

"Ugh," Parker complained, "minimart coffee." She grinned. "But if that's all we can get…" she said, driving off. "Are you referring to the one on the edge of town?"

Felicia nodded.

The women were just returning to the car with their coffee when they heard the squeal of tires on pavement. They looked up to see an old truck slide sideways into the back of Jud's car. Parker groaned, "Oh, no."

"Hey!" Felicia called as the driver backed up and started to drive away. "Hey, you! Stop!"

The driver looked at her, turned, and sped away.

"Well, that was rude," Parker said.

"Rude, indeed," Felicia agreed.

"Darn it all to heck," Parker complained. "Now we have to call the cops."

"We do?" Felicia questioned. "Are you sure that's a good idea in light of what we're doing tonight?"

"Hmmm," Parker muttered. "Good point." She walked around to the back of the car.

"The damage isn't too bad." She looked up. "Wait. That guy's coming back. Shoot, we'd *better* call the cops."

Meanwhile Jud, Raif, and Pamela walked along village streets and through neighborhoods to find the right place from which to send off the drone.

"There," Pamela said. "There's a small park. Let's do it there. No one will see us in that shaded area. Will that work?"

"Perfectly," Raif said. "Yeah, dense shade." He winced. "The drone has small lights on it, but hopefully it won't be noticed."

"Send it off," Jud insisted. "Let's get on with it."

"Okay," Raif said, powering on the drone and manipulating it into the air. He watched his monitor for a few minutes and finally said, "We're almost there."

Jud and Pamela waited silently but anxiously for Raif's next report.

"We're in," Raif whispered. He then said, "Oops."

"What?" Jud demanded.

"Damn," Raif said. "Something's wrong. I just made it over the wall and the picture started to pixelate." He spent several more minutes trying to adjust the thing, when he said, "I'm going to call it back out of there. Oh!" he yelped. "Now it's working. I'll try again, guys."

Once the drone breached the wall, again the picture on his screen became scrambled.

"Damn," Raif huffed, "they must have some sort of technology in there to prevent photography from the air—at least by drone."

Jud blew out a breath in frustration. "Okay, let's get over there and find out for ourselves what's behind wall number one."

"You're going to climb that wall?" Pamela asked.

"If we have to," Jud said. "I think that whatever's inside there is key to us rescuing my daughter and Raif's mom and maybe others."

"Don't forget Olivia," Pamela said.

"The cat?" Raif said. "What's so special about the cat?"

"Oh, don't let Parker hear you say that," Pamela hissed.

Raif looked from Pamela to Jud. When he didn't receive a response, he suggested, "Okay, let's walk." He took a couple of steps, then looked at the drone he held. "Hey, I don't want to carry this thing around, I'll just stash it here. We can get it on our way back."

Jud chuckled. "Aren't you the confident one?"

"What do you mean by that?" Raif asked. "Do you think someone's going to steal it?"

Pamela shook her head and said hesitantly, "I think he means we may not come out of there alive." She shuddered. "Gads, you guys are really going in there?"

"Yeah," Jud said, walking swiftly down the sidewalk with Raif. "Getting cold feet, Pamela?" he asked, as she trotted to catch up. "What are you afraid of? She's not a real witch."

"Yeah, but what if she knows spells? Someone could have taught her spells. And then there are the dogs," Pamela reminded him.

"Would you rather go back and guard the drone alone in that dark park?" Jud teased.

"I'll probably wish I'd taken you up on that," she muttered as she continued walking with the men.

At the same time Jud and the others were creeping around the village, Parker chuckled quietly and said, "Felicia, the guys and my cousin are probably deep in a fascinating investigation about now, while we're stuck with a stupid fender bender. Oh," she said, "here comes a police unit." She waved them over and watched as two officers exited the car and walked toward them.

Parker was about to speak when the other driver leaped from his truck and shouted, "They ran into me! Those two gals came from nowhere and rammed me like they were doing it on purpose. Then they tried to run. It was a hit-and-run. I confronted them and told them to stay here while I called you guys, and the dark-haired one there, she hit me. See, I'm bleeding. She hit me with something. I don't know what it was. I was ambushed, I tell you."

"What?" Parker shrieked. "You jerk! You hit our car while it was parked. Then *you* ran…"

"And before you took off," Felicia said, "I saw your face. You must have hit it on the steering wheel or something. You were all bloody when you drove off."

"She is such a liar!" the man spat. "If I ran, what am I doing here?"

"Okay, okay," one of the officers said. "Calm down." He looked around. "Were there any witnesses?"

"Maybe the store clerk," Parker suggested. "There was a screech of tires before impact, so the clerk might have looked up and saw it."

The officer nodded and said, "Okay, I'm Officer Sandefur, this is Sergeant Carlson. Can I see your registration and license, please, ma'am?" He looked at Parker, then Felicia. "Who was driving?"

"No one," Parker said. "The car was parked right there. We were just coming out of the minimart after getting a cup of coffee." She asked, "May I reach into the car for my purse, and I imagine the registration is in the glove box."

"You imagine?" the officer asked.

"This isn't my car," Parker said.

"And you say you weren't driving?" he continued. "You were coming from the minimart? Then why is your purse in the car?" he asked.

"We sat in there with the doors locked waiting for you," Parker explained.

He nodded and said, "Yeah, go ahead and get your purse and the registration." While the sergeant stood a distance away with the other driver, Officer Sandefur watched Parker gather the documents. She handed them to him, and he asked, "Are you Parker Campbell?" When she nodded, he asked, "Who's Judson Caldwell?"

"A friend," she answered. "This is his car. He asked me to run an errand for him."

Overhearing this, the other driver shouted, "That's not her car? Oh that's just great. She must have stole it?"

"Will you settle down?" Sergeant Carlson said, walking farther away with the man.

"Where does Mr. Caldwell live?" the officer asked.

"He lives in a small berg outside of San Francisco. I'm not even sure of the name," Parker said, feeling quite inadequate and not in control of the moment. "We're working together on a case."

He eyed her suspiciously, and asked, "Where is he?"

"Well, he's doing a little surveillance as we speak," she said. "My friend and I just stopped in to get a cup of coffee because we're picking him up in a little bit…" When the officer didn't respond, she added, "with her brother and my cousin."

He glanced up at her and shook his head dubiously.

"Look," she said, "I'm Parker Campbell…"

"I know, you told me."

"I'm an investigative reporter," she explained. "I travel all over the country working on odd criminal cases and mysteries. You must have heard of me."

"Lady," the officer said, "I'd advise you to stop talking. You're not helping yourself."

"What about Olivia? Do you know Olivia? We work together," she said.

"What, stealing cars?" he asked. He turned to Felicia. "Are you Olivia?"

"No," Parker insisted. "Olivia is a cat." She knew immediately upon seeing the look on Officer Sandefur's face that she was backing herself into a very precarious corner. She shook her head and glanced at Felicia, who was staring at her in horror. "Gads, I'd *better* shut up," Parker murmured, fidgeting.

"What did you get, Mike?" Officer Sandefur asked when his partner approached. He looked at the two women, glanced at the other driver, and led Sergeant Carlson a short distance away.

"What did I get from that guy?" the sergeant repeated, "A lot of rambling accusations." He asked, "Where was their car when this happened?"

"They say it was parked right there," Officer Sandefur said.

The sergeant shined his flashlight around on the ground. "Well, I see skid marks leading right up to where it was hit. Sure looks to me like the girls are telling the truth."

"Really?" Officer Sandefur questioned. He frowned and said quietly to his partner, "I have to tell you, I was leaning in the other direction." He motioned toward Parker. "That one's loony—says she's a crime reporter and her partner is a cat." He laughed. "A cat named Olivia."

The sergeant did a double take and asked, "Is that Parker Campbell? Hey, she's pretty amazing." He looked around. "Is Olivia with her?"

"Are you losing it, man?" Officer Standefur asked. "Oh, tell me you're joking around."

"No. Do you mean you haven't you heard of Parker Campbell?" the sergeant asked. "She writes for all types of publications, and you'll find her articles on the internet. Yeah, she's well-known in the industry. Where have you been, under a rock?"

"Uh…no. So you think the other guy's at fault?"

"Absolutely positively," Sergeant Carlson said.

"Do you want to arrest him or cite him?" Officer Sandefur asked.

"We're taking him in," his partner said. "He's under the influence of something—I don't know what. I found some sort of substance in his car. Yeah, he's looped up on something and spewing

all kinds of stories. None of them make any sense."
He pointed. "Hey, here comes the store clerk. "Let's
see what he has to say." He walked toward the
clerk and introduced himself. "I'm Sergeant Mike
Carlson. Can you tell me what you saw here this
evening?"

"Yeah," the younger man said, "those two
women had just left the store after buying two cups
of coffee when I heard the tires squeal and the
crash. I saw him through the window get out of his
truck, look at the damage, then peel out of here."

"So this car was parked when the crash
occurred," he confirmed. "And where were the
women?"

"Just walking out of the store," the clerk
said. When he saw a couple approaching the
minimart, he turned and said, "That's all I know.
Gotta go."

"Well, Ms. Campbell," Officer Sandefur
said, returning the documents to her, "I owe you an
apology. I'm sorry this has happened to you ladies
and that I didn't believe you, but…"

Parker nodded. "I know. It's been a long day,
and I'm kind of tired—I'm also not used to this sort
of interrogation."

"Where's Olivia?" the sergeant asked, after
cuffing the other driver and helping him into the
patrol car.

"Um…I guess you could say she's on a
case," Parker said, choking up.

"Are you all right, ma'am?" he asked.

She nodded. "Yeah. As I said, it's been a long day."

## Chapter Seven

"Where do you suppose they are now?" Parker asked as she pulled away from the minimart in Jud's car.

"I don't know," Felicia said, "but my coffee's cold, darn it."

"Want to go back in and get a refill?" Parker asked.

Felicia thought for a minute and said, "No. I think we'd better stay away from that place. Hey, is that your phone?"

"Yes, it's in my purse there. Want to see who it is?"

"J. C." Felicia reported once she had the phone in her hands.

"Oh, that's Jud. Answer it, will you?" Parker listened as Felicia had a brief conversation with Jud, then she asked, "Well?"

"I don't know," Felicia said, looking down at the phone. "He whispered mostly. He was saying something about their original plan having failed. The drone failed or something. He asked if we could pick it up at a park just west of the Dunbar place under a couple of shade trees."

"Oh, great—without a flashlight?" Parker complained.

"Hey," Felicia said, turning in her seat, "I saw one in the backseat while we were being interrogated." She chuckled. "I began to worry about what a detective would carry in his car that could get us arrested." She reached for the light and reported, "It works."

"Good," Parker said, making a turn. "What else did Jud say?"

"He said they're going in on foot and taking their chances, then he swore…"

"He swore?" Parker asked.

Felicia nodded. "Yes. He spewed some expletives, then he said something about a car coming. I think I heard Raif say, 'It's a Jag…Mom's Jag.' Then I just heard scuffling or something, like Jud didn't end the call, and he was running, maybe. There was another shout then the phone went dead."

Not sure what to think of Felicia's news, Parker drove slowly down a residential street until she saw what appeared to be a small park. She pulled over. "Get the flashlight; let's see if we can find that drone." Parker started to get out of the car, then stopped. She picked up her phone and said, "Olivia!"

"Where?" Felicia asked, looking around. "Did you see her?"

"No," Parker said, "but I may be able to find out how she is and maybe how to get to her." She shook her head. "Why didn't I think of this before?"

"What?" Felicia asked, clearly confused.

Parker taped her phone screen and explained, "My brother speaks to cats. Why didn't I think of that until now?"

Felicia put a hand on Parker's arm in a calming manner. "Listen, hon, it's been a tense situation for all of us, and frightening. You've been under a lot of stress. We all have. So what is it you think your brother can do to help? Where is he? Does he live in this area?"

Parker shook her head and explained quickly, "No. He's in Colorado, but he can communicate with animals, especially cats." She started to tap her phone screen when Felicia asked, "Do you know what time it is in Colorado?"

Parker thought for a moment, then placed the call. "Yeah, this is too blasted important to wait."

"Parker," came a cranky voice on the other end of her phone, "what are you doing? Did you pocket dial me? It's not even four in the morning, for heaven's sake."

"Oh, I thought you'd be up feeding horses, you wrangler, you."

"Well, I am up, just barely. It's nearly two a.m. there—or are you someplace other than California this week? I heard you were in Frisco."

"Yes, I'm still in the San Francisco area," she said, "and I need your help."

"What did Olivia do now?" he grumbled

"Wade, she has been taken by a witch or a wannabe witch. They think she's somehow sacred or whatever…"

"Olivia?" he questioned.

"Yes, because of her coloring," she explained.

He paused, then asked, "So, do you want me to tell you where she is?"

"No. I know where she is. I need to know how to get past the warlocks and big-fanged dogs to rescue her."

"What?" he almost shouted.

"Wade?" she called out. "Wade, are you there?"

"Yes. Parker, can you be patient?" he scolded. "There's something coming in on another channel."

"You're watching TV?" she shrieked. "Wade, I need your help. This is important."

"Parker, stop talking," he insisted. "It's Olivia. I need to listen for a moment."

"Oh, sorry," she said quietly. She grinned at Felicia and mouthed, "I guess I *am* a bit overwrought."

"Parker," Wade said.

"What?" she managed, hesitantly.

"Olivia is fine. She's being treated like a queen. Actually those weren't her words—she showed me an image of her eating from gold-rimmed bowls. I don't think it's real gold, though. I sense that it's fake." He was quiet for a moment, then said, "Olivia is fine. She's comfortable and happy, only she misses you. Yeah, she's comfortable, but this isn't the lifestyle she prefers—not for the long term. She's ready to come home."

"How can I get to her?" Parker whined.

Wade hesitated, then said, "The opportunity is coming."

"Did you get that from Olivia?" she asked.

"No, actually. It seemed as though it came from another source. I don't know who or what, but here's what I see, for what it's worth: cars. Luxury cars like in a parade. A ship—a cargo ship, maybe. Parker, the opportunity is close." He then said, "Darn! Sorry, that's it."

Wade," she whined.

"She's okay, Parker. You'll be together soon. Gotta go."

Parker ended the call, then stared down at her phone.

"What did he say?" Felicia asked. "Did he talk to Olivia?"

Parker nodded. "He said she's fine, but she misses me." She swallowed hard. "I miss her so much." She thought for a moment, then muttered, "He also said something about cars."

Felicia shook her head. "This is so fascinating. I know a few other people who talk to animals. I think that's just the most fascinating skill or art or gift—I guess it would be considered a gift."

"You told me earlier that you have a gift handed down from your grandmother," Parker said. "Are you psychic or what?"

"I'm not sure what you'd call it." Felicia faced Parker. "In fact, I'm not sure it's anything special. I believe it's something we all have in us. It's called intuition. We all have it, but some of us are apparently born with a greater level of it, or we simply learn to use it at deeper levels. I knew from the time I was quite young that I had some sort of knowingness that my peers didn't seem to have. I thought it made me a freak, so I tried to suppress it. When I learned how valuable—and even fun—it can be I began pursuing it." She giggled. "Like back there at the gas station. I played a little trick on that other driver."

Amused, Parker asked, "What did you do, for heaven's sake?"

"Well, I don't think that guy was under the influence, but I put it into his head that he was so he'd act the part and he'd be arrested and we'd be on our merry way." She laughed. "You sure weren't helping our case any. In fact, you'd think I'd put that thought into *your* head." She gasped. "Parker, do you think I did that to you? You were pretty weird there for a while."

"I don't know," Parker said. "I sure couldn't stop the flow of words, and believe me, I tried."

Felicia slapped her hand over her mouth. "I'm sorry. My grandmother warned me to be careful how I use my gift—to keep a tight rein on it."

As fascinating as Parker found the conversation, she was distracted by something Wade had said. She looked down at her phone again. "Luxury cars like in a parade…cargo ship…"

"What?" Felicia asked. "Luxury cars like in a parade?" she repeated. "Is that what your brother said?" When Parker nodded, she gasped, "Oh my gosh, Parker, I had that same vision."

"When?" Parker asked.

"Off and on all evening, actually."

"Felicia, why didn't you say something?"

"Do you know what it means?" Felicia countered.

Parker shook her head. "Not a clue."

"Neither do I. That's why I didn't verbalize it. But now that your brother did…" She screeched, "and Jud. He said something about a car—Mom's car. Wow! It sounds like we're on the same page, but…"

"Yeah, but," Parker repeated, opening her car door. "Let's go get that drone, then I want to maybe get closer to the Dunbar compound. What do you think?"

"I'm with you," Felicia said.

Several minutes earlier, at the Dunbar compound, Jud had just ended his brief conversation with Felicia. He hissed, "Look out!"

Raif grabbed Pamela and they dove into a shelter of shrubs alongside Jud.

"Wow!" Pamela whispered, watching a procession of cars emerge from behind the wall. "There's our way in."

"Wait," Jud said, stopping her. "Let's see what else comes out of there first." He asked Raif. "Did you say you saw your mom's Jag?"

Raif nodded. "Yes, but dang it, I couldn't see who was driving it. Nor could I see who was driving any of the other cars."

"That's crazy," Pamela said, being careful to stay in the shadows with the men.

They watched another two cars roll out of the enclosure and continue down the street, then Jud said, "Be on the alert, guys. Let's slip in there before the gate closes. When you hear it engage, run like hell. Dive onto the ground or slip around against the wall, whatever you can do to stay hidden." He gave Pamela a shove. "Did you hear that? The gate's closing. Go! Go!"

"Is that a gun?" Pamela whispered seconds later when Jud pulled her to him against the inside wall. "Jud, are you carrying a gun?"

"Of course," he hissed. He asked, "Do you see those dogs anywhere? Is this where you ran into them?"

She shook her head. "No. They're in another enclosure on the other side of this wall."

Once the gate had closed, the trio looked around and Jud said, "Stay put for a few minutes. Let's get the lay of the land from here. It appears they operate the gate from inside that building, maybe. What in the heck is this place?" He nodded. "Hey, I just saw a light go on over there."

"I see it," Raif said. "That looks like some sort of housing. But where in the heck were all those cars kept? That building's too small to hold them."

"Unless," Jud said

"Unless?" Raif questioned.

"Unless they've gone underground. They may have an underground garage, but why?"

"Look!" Pamela hissed, pointing. "It's Olivia. Did you see that? Olivia was just at that window where the light's on."

"I don't see anything," Jud said. "Anyway, how can you be sure it's her—don't all those colorful cats look the same? Parker said she saw some cats like her here earlier today."

"I swear it was Olivia," Pamela insisted. "One night at Parker's condo I couldn't sleep, mostly because that darn cat was playing in my room—wide awake and having a ball playing. By the time she finally settled down, I was wide awake, so I just lay there looking at her. I have that face of hers ingrained in my brain." Pamela glanced at each of the men. "Listen, I tell you that's Olivia. Come on, let's go get her."

"What if that's the witch's quarters?" Raif whispered.

"I can't imagine that," Pamela said. "That's probably where the workers live."

"How will we get her out of here?" Raif asked. "I mean, she's a cat."

"Jud glanced around. "The lighting isn't all that good, but it appears it would be easier to get out than to get in. The drop on the other side is farther down. See how the ground is built up in here—except for the driveway where the cars came through."

"Great—so you think we can get out, but we'll probably break a leg in the process?" Pamela grumbled.

Jud had an idea. "I'll get Parker over here—maybe she and Felicia can find something that will break our fall."

"Now you're daydreaming," Raif said.

Jud looked around. "We might even find something in here that we can toss over the wall to cushion our fall."

"Just so we don't toss it into the dog pen," Pamela said, shuddering. She then said, "Listen, there's nobody around, so I'm going over to that building where I saw Olivia and check it out. I'd love to get my hands on the cat."

"Okay," Jud said. "Come on, Raif."

"I think you're right that it's housing," Jud said as they drew near. "It's a series of small apartments. The light's out now."

"Yeah, but," Pamela said, "whoever is in there won't be asleep yet. Come on."

Jud held her back. "Wait! Maybe you should go by yourself."

"Huh?" she gasped.

"We'll be right outside there if you need help. I believe you might be more successful if you go alone," he explained.

Pamela thought for a moment. "Okay," she said, walking cautiously toward where she'd seen the calico cat. She found a row of doors on the other side of the building. Determined that she'd seen the cat in the third window along the row, she knocked on the third door. Nothing. She knocked lightly again, and that's when she thought she heard someone moving around inside. *It sounds like a child running and playing,* she thought. *Is there a little kid in there?* She knocked one more time and then heard a loud, high-pitched meow. *That's Olivia,* she thought. She started to knock again when a woman's voice called, "Who is it? Is that you, Lucy?"

Unsure of what to do or say, Pamela said, "Yes."

The woman called out, "Lucy, you know I can't get out by myself. Use that key they left out there—the one in that block of wood."

*Block of wood,* Pamela thought. *Oh my gosh, whoever is in there is a prisoner.* She motioned for the two men to join her. Once they did, she whispered, "There's a woman inside and she said she's a prisoner. She thinks I'm Lucy."

"Lucy?" Jud gasped.

"She said there's a key out here in a block of wood. I think you should come in with me."

"Yes," Jud said. He looked around, then pointed. "There." He picked up a piece of wood, pulled it apart, and discovered a key, which he used in the lock.

Pamela opened the door and stepped inside to be greeted rather suspiciously. "You're not Lucy," the woman said. "You told me your name is Lucy."

"It is," Pamela lied. "My name *is* Lucy. Were you expecting a different Lucy?" When the men followed her in and closed the door behind them, Pamela said, "This is Jud and Raif."

"Mom!" Raif almost shouted. He walked closer to the woman. "Mom, what are you doing in here? You say they're holding you against your will?"

"Oh, Son, I'm sorry that you found me. That wasn't supposed to happen until I've finished my work here." More excitedly she said, "I've been invited to work with the high priestess." She clasped her hands under her chin. "What an honor. She said I have a gift." The woman giggled. "A gift, Raif." She tilted her head and asked, "What are you doing here, anyway? How did you find me, and who are these people?" She backed away. "I don't think you're supposed to be in here." She rushed to the window and pulled the drapes closed. "Although there aren't many people on the grounds right now. Lucy told me they were almost all going someplace this evening."

"So there's no one in the compound?" Jud asked.

She looked suspiciously at him. "I suppose there is someone, but a lot of them left on a mission. That's why Lucy—" she looked at Pamela. "—the other Lucy—brought me the magical cat. That cat," she said pointing to Olivia. "Lucy could tell when she brought me my dinner that I was sad. I miss my cats, and they won't let me out to play with the cats that frolic among the herb gardens. Oh, and they took my phone so I can't call anyone." She grinned. "It's all part of the teaching here. The isolation helps us to focus. It's been kind of hard sometimes," she smiled, "but Lucy is so kind."

When the calico cat walked up to Pamela and rubbed against her leg, she said, "Hi, Olivia." She leaned over and petted her. "It's sure good to see you."

The woman frowned. "Olivia? Her name is not Olivia, it's Vivienne. Isn't she a lovely cat? And she cheered me up like you wouldn't believe."

"Mom," Raif said, taking her arm. He led her to a small sofa and sat down with her. "Mom, I'm quite sure they've stolen your car…"

"What" she asked. "My car? How? Why?"

"I don't know. I'm concerned about your bank accounts too. We'll put a stop to any transactions first thing in the morning."

"Why, Son? Who are you talking about? What are you implying?"

"You've been swindled, Mom," he said gently.

"No," she asserted, "that can't be."

"Mom, I believe they're running a scam here."

"No," she insisted, "everyone's been so nice and they've treated me well."

"We just saw someone drive your car and a bunch of other cars off the property," Raif explained, "and the plates have been changed. I noticed that your DivaDoris plates weren't on the car."

"Then it probably wasn't my car," Doris reasoned.

220

"It *was* your car," Raif insisted. "Remember that little sticker Felicia put on your bumper as a joke when you first bought the car—the one that says, *Purr*? It's still there, Mom."

"Oh, dear. I wonder if the high priestess knows about this," Doris mumbled.

"I'd bet she's the brains behind it," Raif said.

"What should I do?" Doris whined, wringing her hands. "Oh my gosh, I feel like I'm in one of those cartoon movies where nothing is as it seems— like in the *Wizard of Oz*." She shook her head. "I notice that my brain has become kind of foggy since I've been here, so that doesn't help."

"I'm sure that's arranged through the drinks, food, ventilation system, and maybe rituals— hypnotic rituals," Pamela explained.

Doris slumped against the back of the sofa. "Oh, my." She put her hand on Raif's arm. "You won't tell Felicia about this will you?"

"He grinned. "Too late, Mom. She's the one who brought me up here. She knew something was wrong. We've been here for a couple of days looking for you—trying to figure out what happened to you."

Just then Jud returned from another room after having made a couple of phone calls. He announced, "I sent the police to the docks, where I suspect the cars are being taken, and I called Parker.

They're just outside the property, here. They're looking for a way out for us."

"Out of this area?" Doris asked. "Goodness, all you have to do is push the button and the gate opens. I watch them out the window. That gate doesn't open often, but it's interesting to watch it slide. That's a big gate—an invisible gate, right?"

"It sure is," Jud agreed. "It just looks like part of the wall."

"And it rolls open right into the wall," Doris said.

Jud smiled. "So you know where the button is? Ma'am, I could kiss you."

Doris grinned coyly. "I just might let you."

"Mom!" Raif scolded.

"So where is the button?" Jud asked. He held out his hand. "By the way, I'm Jud, and you are?"

"Doris," she said, walking to the window. She opened the drape slightly and pointed. "See that blue boxed-in area or wall or whatever it is against that building? There must be a way to open the gate from behind it. I see people go behind it, then the gate opens. Give it a try."

"You're going with us, Mom," Raif said. "Get your things. Do you have jewelry or anything you want to take with us? You usually wear a lot of it, where is it?"

Doris said, matter-of-factly, "It's with the high priestess. She said it's important for me to

222

shed the unnecessary, impractical, and fake parts of myself during my induction."

"Induction?" Raif snarled. "Induction into what?"

"The next level," Doris said. "We're on different levels, you see, depending on how aware we are, and intuitive." She smiled broadly and boasted, "I've reached the next-to-highest level." She added, "Anyway, she has my belongings for safekeeping."

"Yeah, I'll just bet she does," Raif said sarcastically. "So you don't have anything here with you?"

"Just my toothbrush and one change of clothes," Doris admitted.

"Well, get dressed, Mom," Raif instructed. "You can wear my jacket. It's cold out there."

"Pamela," Jud asked, "can you hold onto the cat? We don't have a harness for her. We sure don't want her to get away."

"I think I'll be okay. She seems calm and easy to handle," Pamela said.

"Wrap a towel around her," Doris suggested. "I'll get a towel. I think that's safer." She took a few steps back. "Wait, you can't take Vivienne. Lucy will be coming back for her. I don't want Lucy to get into trouble."

"Don't you understand, Mom?" Raif said. "You could be in danger if you stay here. All of us could be."

"And we believe the cat could be in danger, too," Pamela said.

Raif nodded. "Now get dressed and let's go, Mom."

"Yes," Jud said, peeking through a slit between the drape panels, "before that bunch gets back."

By then Parker and Felicia were on the compound grounds. Parker hissed, "Look! The gate's opening. Stay hidden. We don't know who in the heck's coming out of there."

"I'm hiding," Felicia said. After a few moments, she pointed and whispered, "Look, there's Raif with Mom…"

"And Pamela," Parker said quietly. She slapped her hand over her mouth and squealed, "She has Olivia. Oh, thank goodness, she has Olivia." She stood up and motioned to the others as they darted through the open gate. "Where's Jud?" she asked, urging the others to hunker down with her and Felicia in the shrubbery.

"Hitting the *close* button," Raif said. "I hope he can make it out of there."

"Here he comes," Pamela said. She cringed and mouthed, "Hurry, Jud. Hurry."

"Gads," he said, diving into the bushes with the others seconds later, "they have that thing set so it's nearly impossible to sneak out. Did you see how far away they put that mechanism?" He blew out a breath. "I haven't run that fast in…"

"Gimme, gimme," Parker begged, holding her hands out to Pamela and taking Olivia into her arms.

At the same time Felicia hugged her mother. "Mom," she murmured, "are you okay? Where were you? How…?"

"I don't know what all the fuss is about," Doris said, pulling back. "I've been having a good time, meeting nice people, having delicious meals."

"While they're stealing her car, her jewelry, and probably her bank accounts," Raif growled.

"Where's your purse, Mom?" Felicia asked. "And don't you have an overnight bag?"

"Like I told your brother, they're holding all of that for me. It's nonessential to the program here. You know, not something I need, because I'll be going into an altered state where our reality is. Where we live is fake, you see. Reality is in the inner workings of our mind, on another plane." Doris frowned and added, "Or something like that."

Raif shook his head. "So you handed over your purse with your driver's license, social security card…what else, Mom?"

"Well, my phone is in there, of course…"

"Oh, Mom," Felicia complained.

Meanwhile, Parker snuggled with Olivia and kissed her little head. "I was so worried about you," she crooned.

"She's purring," Pamela said, smiling.

"Listen, we'd better get out of here before…" Jud hissed. Suddenly he crouched and muttered, "Uh-oh."

They heard a man's voice call, "Who's there? What do you want? Hey, come out of there."

"Where's the car?" Jud whispered.

"Up the street, about three-quarters of a city block," Parker said quietly.

"Okay, gang," Jud hissed, grabbing both Parker's and Pamela's arms, "run for it." He guided them out into the open toward the driveway, then heard someone shout.

"Stop!"

Suddenly, they heard what sounded like a shot.

"Holy, sh…" Jud started. He glanced behind him and saw Raif and Felicia running toward them, one on each side of their mother. Before he knew what had happened, something stopped his forward motion and he, along with the others, fell to the ground. They tried, but were unable to get up.

"It's a damn net," Jud said, trying to get free of it. "Does anyone have a knife?"

"Never mind that," a man snarled. "Just stay put until we get someone out here who can deal with you."

"Olivia!" Parker shouted. "I lost my grip on her when I fell." She could see the cat in the dim light pushing against the net. "Grab her. Can

226

someone grab her? No, Olivia!" Parker cried, trying to crawl toward the cat, but it was too late. Olivia had found a hole just large enough to push through, and she trotted off into the darkness. "Oh no," Parker whined.

"What's happened?" another man asked, running toward the net with two others.

"Hmmm," Doris muttered. "There are more people here than I thought."

"Well, there will be five less people in a short while," one man said. "Trespassing and breaking out are punishable by death, unless we have room in the underground prison."

When Pamela looked at Parker with fear in her eyes, Parker squeezed her cousin's hand.

Suddenly the weight of the net lifted, seemingly by hydraulic means, and the four men rushed in, shouting, "Get up! All of you, get up!" As they pushed and shoved the four women and two men toward a back door of the main building, one of the captors remarked, "The car brigade is back."

Jud glanced behind him and saw a group of men and women, all dressed in long cloaks, marching into the compound. One of them called out, "Hey, what's going on?"

"Interlopers," one of the captors said. "We're taking them to the torture and execution room."

Jud watched as the returning group, consisting of about a dozen people, continued their trek toward the big gate, all except for one. *What's she doing?* he wondered. *She broke away from the others, and they didn't seem to notice.* He faced ahead where they were being led and thought, *Sheesh, here I am about to be tortured and maybe executed, and I'm curious about why one of the residents or helpers is behaving oddly. Yeah, I'd better pay attention to what's going on here, so I can get us out of this mess. They haven't found my handgun, so I still have an advantage, but there are four of them, and I sure don't want any of us to get hurt.*

Parker looked around, trying to catch a glimpse of Olivia. *So close yet so far,* she thought. *And now—oh my gosh, what's going to happen now? Oh, Olivia, I'm so sorry.* She felt a rush of tears burning her eyes.

"The torture and execution room," one of the captors announced, leading them into a dark, dismal room. "I'll ring for Effie," he said. "She loves to watch these things."

"This time of morning?" another young man asked. "Let's chain them, rough them up, then we'll schedule the main event for after breakfast."

The other men chortled. One called out, "Sounds good to me." He then asked, "Hey, where'd that cat come from. Isn't that Effie's new cat? Ouch!" he shouted.

"What's wrong with you?" another man asked.

He screamed, "The cat's got me! Get it off me! Get it off me!" he hollered, struggling to hold tightly to Parker and Pamela while avoiding Olivia's wrath.

Just as he prepared to kick at Olivia, another man shouted, "You'd better not hurt that cat. It's Effie's latest conquest. You know how she likes to win against a mulish cat. You harm that cat before Effie triumphs, and she'll bring you down to this chamber. You know she will. Remember what happened to Timothy and Paul?"

"Ouch," the man screeched again. "I don't care how sacred Effie considers that cat, I'm not going to take a clawing," he said, pushing Parker and Pamela away from him and sliding a steel rod from a sheath on his belt. He raised it threateningly above his head and snarled, "I'll kill you, cat."

Parker fell up against the wall and shrieked, "Nooo!" She hid her face in her hands, feeling utterly helpless.

Suddenly a female voice rang out. "Stop! Stop this now!" she bellowed.

The captors turned to see who spoke. One man said, "It's only Lucy. Come to watch the fun, Lucy?"

"Yes," she said, "but let *me* have the pleasure of destroying the cat."

"*You* destroying a cat?" the man questioned.

"Yes!" she said, picking up Olivia. "She's nothing but trouble, and she has Effie off kilter—

you know her flow has been interrupted, and I think it's because of this evil cat. Please, let me take care of her."

"Nooo!" Parker shouted.

"Quiet," the man closest to her demanded. He then said, "Really, Lucy? What will you tell Effie?"

"That it was an accident," she said, lightly.

He grinned at her. "Okay. Sure, take the cat and do what you will. Then come back here and watch the fun we're going to have."

Lucy grinned. "Sure, Boyd. Thanks." She hurried out of the room with Olivia in her arms.

Parker felt such a burden of grief that she thought she'd be sick, but she fought hard against it. *We just have to find a way out of this,* she thought, *and the sooner the better. Maybe we can catch Lucy before…oh, God, please let me wake up from this nightmare.*

The four men were discussing how they would proceed when Lucy returned. She moved to the back of the room and howled, "Let them go. Let them go, now!"

A couple of the men laughed at her and one said, "Let them go, you say? You're going to stop us? How?" he asked.

"She's joking," another man said. He ordered, "Proceed!"

Lucy spoke more loudly. "I don't think so, Brad. How will I stop you, you ask? With this," she said, revealing a small vial of liquid.

"Is that…?" Brad asked, stepping back with fear in his eyes. "Where did you get that?"

"I thought I might need it some time," she explained sweetly, "so I took it a few weeks ago when Effie was feeling poorly. I just had this feeling I might need it, so while everyone was fawning over Effie, I grabbed it." She grinned. "I've been eager to give it a try."

"You'll kill us all," Brad said, weakly.

"Don't you want to see how it works?" Lucy asked. "I mean, Effie's been telling us about it and threatening us with it for years. Shall we try it out?"

"Don't push her, Brad," another man said, backing up against a wall. "She's been acting strange lately. Effie's been concerned that she would turn on us. Lucy, what happened? Why are you doing this?"

Without responding, she continued holding the vial over her head and demanded, "Let them go."

One by one the men released their grip on their prisoners, and Lucy said to them, "Go. Leave while you can."

Before Jud and the others reached the door, however, one of the men blocked their escape.

Lucy grinned at him, dangled the vial over her head between two fingers, and said, "Good bye, Tad."

"No," he said, moving away from the door.

"Good. Okay, all of you warlocks, up against the wall over there. Now!" she shouted.

"What's wrong with you?" Tad screeched.

"Nothing," Lucy said, looking at Jud. "Finally I'm seeing things clearly." She motioned to the prisoners. "Go. There's nothing stopping you. Go!"

Raif, took his mother's arm, nudged his sister, and he led the way out of the room. Parker and Pamela followed.

"Jud," Parker said, when he hesitated.

"Go!" Lucy shouted. Once the others were outside, Lucy continued to hold the vial threateningly as she followed them out, locking the door behind her. "Run!" she hissed.

Parker slowed and called out, "Olivia!" She stopped and insisted, "I'm not leaving without her."

Lucy caught up to Parker, took her arm, and whispered, "Olivia is safe." When Parker pulled back, Lucy said, "I put her in Dad's car. Come on!"

"Bless you," Parker said, hastening her pace again.

"Where's the damn car?" Jud asked, following the others.

"Just up the street a ways," Lucy said.

"I saw it parked there on our way back from the docks." She looped her arm in Jud's, and pointed. "That's your rattletrap up the street, isn't it, Dad? I can't believe you still have that old thing."

Jud couldn't hold back. He pulled his daughter to him and the pair continued trotting swiftly toward the car. "I like that old car," he said, his voice cracking.

Parker handed him the keys and opened a back door. "There's my girl. Oh, Olivia," she cried, scooping her up into her arms. She stepped back with the cat and said, "Pile in, everyone."

"Yeah, let's get out of here," Jud hissed.

"All of us?" Doris asked.

"We don't have far to go," Felicia said. "Smaller people can sit on bigger people's laps."

"Reminds me of my high-school days," Pamela chuckled as she climbed into the car behind Doris and Felicia.

"Raif, sit up front here," Jud suggested. "Hannah... um... Lucy can sit on your lap. She's small."

Before she got into the car with everyone else, Lucy tossed the vial into a patch of weeds.

"Good God," Jud said.

"Whew!" Raif mumbled. "I thought we were goners."

Lucy laughed and chirped, "Oh, do you mean that vial? It was just water."

"Not funny," Jud complained.

No one spoke for several moments until Pamela pointed. "There go the cops. Are they going to the Dunbar compound?"

"I'm sure they are," Jud said, "and to the docks, where I imagine those people took the cars."

Everyone looked at Lucy, who nodded.

"Shouldn't we answer some questions?" Parker asked. "Won't the police want to interrogate us?"

"Most likely," Jud said. "They know how to reach me. I think they'll be busy at the compound for a while, though."

"I can't believe I'm free," Lucy said as she climbed out of the car. She looked at the bungalow and asked, "Who lives here?"

"Felicia and Raif rented it while they searched for their mother," Pamela explained, walking with the others into the house. Lucy seemed befuddled, so Pamela suggested, "I guess we should introduce ourselves." She pointed, "That's Raif and Felicia."

"Oh yes, I sat on Raif's lap, didn't I?" Lucy said. She looped her arm in Doris's and asked, "Are these your kids, Dori?"

Doris nodded. "Yes, aren't they great—I mean, coming up here to rescue me and all?"

"Yes," Lucy agreed. She looked at Pamela

and Parker. "Are you two sisters?"

"We're cousins," Parker said.

Lucy tilted her head. "I saw you come in with Olivia. I could tell how much you love her, and she loves you, too. The poor thing. Effie surrounded her with luxury," she scowled, "before starting the conquest."

"Conquest?" Parker questioned, holding tightly to Olivia.

Lucy glanced at the others and said quietly, "Her whole thing is to conquer, and cats are some of her favorite victims." She ruffled the fur around Olivia's neck and smiled into her eyes, saying, "Olivia had a lot of admirers, didn't you, precious girl?" She looked up at Parker. "But I could tell, she just wanted to be with you. I'm so glad we got her out of there before…" She blew out a breath, then changed the subject. She looked at Jud. "I saw the two of you and Olivia in town. What's the deal, Dad? Are you dating?"

He grinned and shook his head. "No, Hannah. No dating. Parker helped me sort out what happened that night you and so many others disappeared."

"And Olivia," Parker said. "Olivia helped."

"Yes, and the cat," Jud said begrudgingly.

"Thanks, Dad," Lucy said.

"For coming to your rescue?" he asked.

"For that, of course, but also for bringing me back to being Hannah. You used my name a while ago. That's the first time I've heard it in…"

Jud looked at the date on his watch, and choked up. "It's been seven years to the day."

"Seven years," she repeated. She began to remove the cloak and the dress, revealing a pair of holey jeans and a t-shirt.

Jud watched this and laughed. "There's my girl."

"Yes, I'm Hannah again. No more Lucy and no more Effie."

Pamela pointed at Hannah's feet and asked, "Whose cute little pink shoes are those, Hannah's or Lucy's?"

"Definitely Hannah's," she said.

Parker smiled at her, reached into her tote bag, and pulled out a heavy cardigan sweater. "Here," she said, handing it to Hannah. "You're going to need a wrap this evening."

Hannah smiled. "Thank you. She glanced around at everyone. "You're all so nice." She slipped into the sweater, wrapped her arms around herself, then walked across the room and fell into her father's arms. It was several minutes before she pulled back, smiled into his face, and said, "I missed you, Popsie."

"I missed you, too, Hannah Banana."

The two of them laughed through happy tears and hugged again.

"I can't wait to get home," Hannah said moments later. She grinned. "I hope you haven't changed things around there too much."

Jud shook his head. "You'll find that very little has changed since…" He took her by the shoulders, looked into her eyes, and said, "The only thing missing, Hannah, is your mother."

"I know," she said. When he looked surprised, she explained, "We had access to newspapers. It's one of the underground pleasures we engaged in when we missed our former life."

"Underground?" he asked.

"Yeah," Hannah said, "Effie didn't want us to be informed. It took me a while to realize the hold she had on me—on all of us."

"How?" Jud asked. "Was it drugs?"

Hannah shook her head. "It was more like mind manipulation. Effie—you know, you met her as High Priestess Seraphina—well, she spent years perfecting her methods in hypnosis and mind-control and who knows what all. We got a dose of her manipulation and, well, probably brainwashing every morning. She chortled. "Effie called it rejuvenation. She said she was transforming us into healthier beings—that we were closer to the Supreme Being than anyone on the street or in any religious sect."

"Hannah," Felicia said, "how did you break away?" She added, "I mean from the power of Effie's spell?"

"Yeah," Doris said, "you don't seem—you know, affected like some of the others."

Hannah grinned. "I learned to fake it." She looked at Jud. "I saw you once, Dad, when we were on a mission not too far from home, and I saw how much you'd aged..."

"I aged?" he countered.

"You just looked old to me, and sad. That wore on me. I knew that I was at least partially responsible for that, and I vowed to find a way to fix it. I did. I figured out how to avert or avoid Effie's rhetoric." She glanced at Felicia, "or spell. I became stronger than her crazy programming. I learned to block it and avoid taking any of it in. As I became more clearheaded, I began to devise a plan of my own."

"When was this, Hannah?" Parker asked.

Hannah reached out and petted Olivia. She smiled when Olivia stepped onto her lap and lay down. "This was about six months ago, I'd say."

"Why in the hell didn't you just come home?" Jud demanded.

"You don't understand, Dad. I couldn't. No one can just leave Effie. It's not healthy. I'd learned how to circumvent her programming, but that wasn't enough. I had to somehow take her down or..."

"Did you have help?" Parker asked. "Were any of the others—you know, clearheaded, too?"

"I'm not sure. I didn't talk to anyone about it. That would have been too dangerous. I just kept quiet and waited for the right moment and the right opportunity to…well, I didn't know what I would do or how things would go down." She glanced around. "You people were awesome. The timing was right, and you shook things up just enough to make it happen. I doubt Effie will survive what went down tonight."

"She won't survive?" Doris asked. "Oh, that would be a shame. She is such a great teacher."

"She's a fake, Mom," Raif said.

Appearing to take offense, Hannah said, "Oh no, Raif. She's not a fake, but she is dangerous— evil, conniving, and dangerous. You know that vial I had earlier?"

Raif nodded and said suspiciously, "You said it was water. What did the others think it was?"

"Something Effie put together. She has a chemistry background, and she worked for years to mix a…"

"An explosive?" Felicia asked.

Hannah shook her head. "Worse. Oh, it could blow things up and kill, but it could also cause nerve damage. She wanted something that would have a lasting effect on anyone she chose to use it on. So if you're close enough to it when it goes off and if you aren't killed, you're bound to live in awful pain for the rest of your life." She took a breath. "At least that's how Effie described it to us, which is another reason why no one tries to escape from the compound."

"Where does she keep that stuff?" Jud asked. "We need to let the authorities know about it."

Hannah frowned. "It's not at the compound."

"But those men in the torture chamber thought that's what you had," Pamela said.

"I know," Hannah agreed. "Everyone is told that it's on the compound, but I was probably closer to Effie than anyone, and I know that she didn't want that stuff anywhere around her. She was paranoid as hell…"

She looked at Jud. "Sorry Dad. I know you don't like me to swear." She continued, "Effie had round-the-clock guards who were supposed to be always ready to bring a vial or two of the stuff to the compound. She didn't even tell me where she keeps it, but I don't think it's too far from there."

"Interesting," Parker said. "So you think it's in the neighborhood? Does she own other property in the area?"

"I don't know," Hannah said, "but I think it might be in a particularly vulnerable spot. I've heard her brag about her brilliant decision. She says she has the perfect place for it and built-in guards. She told me more than once that no one knows how close they are to her wrath when they…" Hannah gasped and said more slowly and deliberately, "…when they are baring their soul. The church!" she shouted. This startled Olivia, and she jumped down to the floor. Hannah stood up and turned around,

240

saying, "Oh my gosh, she hid it in the foundation of that new church they built just around the corner there a few years ago. The pastor lives there. They have living quarters and there are facilities for the homeless with—you know, a manager who stays there twenty-four-seven." She gazed around the room. "Do you suppose?"

"I'd better make a call," Jud said. "The local police need to know about this."

## Chapter Eight

"Thank you for making breakfast, Doris and Felicia," Parker said later that morning.

"It's the least we could do after all you've done for us," Felicia said.

Parker patted Raif on the shoulder. "And thank you for the grocery-store run. Olivia was getting tired of kibbles. I didn't think I'd need a supply of canned food when I packed for her yesterday."

"Sure," Raif said, ruffling the fur on Olivia's neck as she sat on the back of the sofa looking up at him. "The gals needed stuff to make breakfast. It was no problem." He smiled. "I'm glad she liked the flavor I picked out. So she's not a finicky cat?"

"Yes, she can be," Parker admitted. She perked up. "Hey, Jud and Hannah are back. How'd it go?" she asked.

Everyone converged on the living room to hear their report, but Doris suggested, "Let's let them eat, shall we? I kept the bacon and sausage warm. I'll scramble you some eggs. Come on, get a glass of juice and a cup of coffee, you two. Wash up," she said, "sit down. Do you want one or two pieces of toast?"

"Bacon, sausage, scrambled eggs, toast," Jud repeated, walking into the kitchen and washing his hands in the sink. "Sounds wonderful."

Hannah chose to freshen up in the bathroom. When she returned, she poured herself and her dad a glass of juice and placed them on the table, asking, "Can I help with anything, Dori?"

Doris hugged her and said, "Just sit down and relax, honey."

Several minutes later, Jud pushed away from the table.

Hannah took her last swig of coffee, saying, "Oh, that was nice…fresh eggs, sausage, strawberry jam on whole-wheat toast. Am I in heaven?"

Everyone laughed and Parker was quick to ask, "So what happened?"

They all gathered around to listen.

"Well, my baby girl was right…" Jud started.

"Daaad," Hannah complained.

He winked at her. "The evil brew was under the church, and the caretaker for the homeless was in charge. I guess there was one other person who knew about this and who was on call to deliver it to the witch if the caretaker wasn't available."

"How would they get to it if it was buried under the church?" Pamela asked.

"Good question," Parker complimented.

"They had devised a hatch of some sort for easy access," Jud explained. He added, "Hidden from view, of course."

"Had she picked up the red phone?" Raif asked. When Jud and Hannah looked at him quizzically he clarified, "Did the witch send for some of that stuff—you know, with the compound being raided and all?"

Jud shook his head. "As far as we know, she hasn't. A HAZMAT crew is removing it from the church premises right now."

"Whew, that's a relief," Doris said.

"It sure is," Hannah agreed. More softly, she added, "I'd sure hate to see something happen to all those innocents."

"Innocents?" Parker questioned.

"There are six or seven other victims housed behind the wall, then there are the people who did Effie's dirty work—they're victims just like I was. Effie took advantage of us all for her own selfish pleasures. She was addicted to power, no matter who it terrorized or inconvenienced or harmed." Hannah shook her head. "Now she'll just be another prisoner in jail."

"So they arrested her?" Felicia asked.

"Damn right," Jud grumbled. "And, Ms. Doris, your car has been recovered!"

"And my purse and…"

"I'm not sure about that," Jud said. "I suppose the officials will confiscate everything they find around there and eventually return it to the rightful owners. Best that you make a claim with the local police department for a quicker return of your items. They'll want your statement, anyway."

"Certainly," Doris said. She frowned. "But I rather liked the woman. Effie made me feel like I had powers and worth."

Felicia and Raif looked at each other and rolled their eyes.

Hannah patted Parker's hand. "Oh, and animal control is out there rescuing all of the cats. Dad told me about the place outside the city where the feral cats can live their life out." She pulled a card from her jeans pocket and handed it to Parker. "Do you want to make that happen? This is the contact number for the assistant director."

"Sure do," Parker said. "I'll make a few calls. Thank you." She moved closer to the young woman and asked, "Hannah, do you mind answering a few questions for me?"

"I have one, too," Pamela said. She looked at Jud, then Hannah. "Why would a church store something for a witch—something dangerous, at that?"

Hannah laughed. "It had to do with her disguises. Effie loved to disguise herself and blend in at local gatherings, the farmers market, the county fair, the grocery store, and even church."

Jud said, "Yeah, evidently the pastor knew nothing about this stuff being stored on the church grounds. The old woman did attend church sometimes, but the people who monitored the vials…"

"Those at the other end of the red phone?" Raif asked.

Jud chuckled and nodded. "Yes, they were plants, handpicked by Effie."

The room grew quiet as everyone tried to assimilate the information, then Hannah asked Parker, "You have questions? Dad told me you write about crimes and mysteries."

Parker nodded and asked soberly, "You were there the night the mudslide occurred, weren't you?"

Lucy slumped. "Yes. It must have happened right after I left with Brad and Travis. We went back to get my purse—I can't believe I left it up there. That's when we knew something had happened."

"Why didn't you come forward with what you saw?" Jud asked. "It's not like you to walk away without reporting something like that. People died, Hannah."

"I know that now. By the time I found out the magnitude of the tragedy, I was already under Effie's influence." She spoke more quietly. "Like I told you, I haven't been myself for a good part of the last seven years. I cannot believe it took me this long to finally retrieve remnants of who I was." She looked at Jud. "What took you so long to find me? Didn't you see the note I left?"

Jud choked up. "Yes, about three weeks ago."

"What?" she yelped, standing up. "I left that message on Mom's phone years ago."

When Parker could see that Jud was struggling with his emotions, she explained to Hannah, "He just recently listened to that message. By the time Olivia found your secret hiding place…"

Hannah reached out for the cat and cradled her face in her hands. "You found it? You are one smart kitty-cat." She kissed Olivia on top of the head.

Jud nodded. "So we just started searching for you a week or ten days ago." He choked up. "I can't believe you're here, Hannah. It's been so long."

"I know, Daddy," she said, sitting down next to him. She wrapped her arms around him and he patted and rubbed her back.

Jud looked across the room at Parker and glanced at Felicia. "By the way, ladies, I'd like an explanation."

"About what?" Parker asked.

"What in tarnation happened to my car?" he demanded. "What did you back into, for cripe's sake?"

Parker made eye contact with Felicia, who stood up and joked, "How about I get you a glass of bourbon?"

Ignoring her, he challenged, "What happened?"

"I'll tell you about it later," Parker said. "I'd like to ask Hannah a few more questions." She looked at Hannah. "If you don't mind."

Hannah, however, was more interested in Olivia at the time. "Oh that's so cute," she gushed when Olivia reached up with one paw on her leg and waved the other paw in the air toward her. "What does this mean?" she asked, laughing. "Is she waving at me?"

Savannah chuckled. "I think she's trying to pet you. She does that to me and it seems to me she's petting or patting me. It is cute, isn't it?"

Hannah nodded. "Charming. I love it. I've never had a cat do that before." She patted her lap and Olivia jumped up. Hannah snuggled with her, then said in a more serious tone, "You know, she came to get me when she knew you were in danger."

"Olivia did?" Parker asked, taking a ragged breath.

Hannah nodded. "That's why she got away from you. She came to me for help."

"Oh! Olivia," Parker said quietly, smiling at the cat.

"She's quite a cat, this one," Hannah said. "I love cats, but I've never met one like her. She and I bonded in a very special way. I knew she was different, and she must have known she could trust me." She raised her face to the sky. "Everything is more wonderful and clear to me now. I'm so grateful to have blessed clarity."

"So you say it was the sessions with Effie that were causing you to be all foggy-headed?" Doris asked.

"I guess—the hypnosis, the hypnotic dance, the conditioning—it was a killer. It took away so much from me and I didn't even notice it, until I met Aurora."

"Aurora?" Parker repeated.

Hannah grinned. "Yeah. Actually, her name is Misty, but Effie thought she needed a spirit name. She came to us recently to be part of Effie's band of followers and worker bees." She grinned. "Effie tried to change my name to Salem, but the others still called me Lucy because of my drawings. Anyway, I didn't know that Aurora had powers, and she used them behind Effie's back. She taught me how to avert the hypnosis therapy that Effie administered every day to keep us under her control. I had no idea how controlled I was until Aurora taught me how to block Effie's programming."

"Well, I hope the police are finding enough infractions of the law to close that bunch down for good," Jud said.

"Still keeping to the letter of the law, huh, Dad?" Hannah asked. She chuckled. "I do believe we were breaking a couple of laws when we all piled into your car last night—or I guess that was this morning." She glanced around. "I don't think anyone was wearing a seat belt."

Ignoring her, he asked, "Hannah, are you willing to tell the police what you know?"

"Do you mean about the thieving, scamming, kidnapping, torturing…" She kissed Olivia and added, "catnapping and all that was going on at that dungeon of horrors?" She nodded. "Absolutely. Yes. I will tell everything I know. I'd like nothing better than to see that evil wannabe high priestess shut down. Dad, we can't have someone like that running scams, taking people's cats and other personal belongings, holding people hostage," she asserted. "Not now that I know what I know."

"Pamela did a high five with Hannah, and Jud choked up, saying, "Welcome back, Hannah. How I've missed you, spunky-girl!"

"Spunky girl," she repeated. "I haven't heard that in a long while." She faced him. "I'm sorry, Dad. I guess I lost my way. I should never have gone with Brad and Travis. I pretty much knew it was wrong from the beginning. By the time I was certain, it was too late. I was under their grandmother's spell."

"How did that happen, anyway?" Felicia asked. "What would make an obviously smart, resourceful, confident young lady like yourself fall under her spell?"

Hannah slumped. "As I said, it was days or maybe weeks after I went to the Dunbar house that we learned the magnitude of the tragedy on the hillside. We'd all gone there to listen to a band that night, but we left early. We knew there had been a slide because, as I said, we went back to get my purse. I never did find it."

Before she could continue, Jud said quietly, "I have it."

"What?" Hannah said, stunned.

"I found it out there where the cats live. That's where the mud came down."

Hannah shook her head. "Oh, that's weird."

"So you didn't find out about the loss of lives until later?" Parker prompted.

"No," Hannah said. "We just knew the road had been washed out." Her voice was subdued when she added, "We found out later that some of my friends were missing. I knew that they were probably dead and that hit me hard. Thinking back, I'm pretty sure that's what made me so vulnerable to Effie's spells. Effie and I came together just at the right time—for her, anyway—for her purposes."

Hannah glanced around at the others. "Effie wanted to build a reputation in the world of the occult. As it turned out, I was the perfect subject for her to induct into her coven or whatever it's called. I was grieving and so needy. Looking back, the kindness and comfort she offered, which now I know was actually her way to manipulate me, was something I needed. I became her lady in waiting. She relied on me for a lot of her personal needs. Because I was so vulnerable in my grief, she was able to take advantage of me for her own benefit." She thought for a moment and said, "When I learned that Mom had died, I went even deeper into my grief, and Effie was there, willing and able to make me feel better." She added, "Actually it's more a matter of no feeling—sort of rising above the emotion." She shook her head. It's hard to explain, but the truth is I trusted her, and I fell under her spell."

"And you found your way out from under it and back home," Jud said. "Thank the Lord, you found your way home."

"And Olivia," Hannah said, ruffling the cat's fur. "Thanks to Olivia, and Parker, and Pamela, and you, Dad."

"What a wild ride." Pamela said later that morning as she rode back to the condo with Parker and Olivia. "I'm drained, emotionally, physically, and intellectually." She grasped Parker's arm. "Thank you for letting me be a part of this. I've never felt so exhausted and exhilarated at the same time." She tilted her head. "Passion. I think I feel that passion you mentioned a couple of days ago. Wow! What an overwhelming sensation."

Parker smiled. "You really were touched, were you?"

"Absolutely," Pamela said. "I felt so alive, valued, and useful." She asked, "Is that what it is to feel the passion you talked about?"

"Kind of, yes," Parker said. "That's certainly part of it."

"Well, that was invigorating, and exciting, and satisfying, but I'm not sure I felt passion. I can say there were some sparks—you know, electricity."

"And sparks can become passion if ignited," Parker explained.

"Whoa," Pamela said, shaking her head, "this is getting deep."

Parker grinned at her cousin and asked, "So, can you see yourself doing that sort of thing as a career?"

"What," Pamela asked, tongue-in-cheek, "breaking and entering, kidnapping old gals, sneaking around to catch someone in a compromising position, plotting against them, taking advantage of circumstances, lying to get my way?" She laughed. "Sure, I could get down with doing that stuff." She tilted her head. "What career would that be, Parker? I can't even imagine."

"Well, Mom and I agree that maybe you should enroll in the police academy," Parker said.

"What?" Pamela chirped. "Me a police officer?"

"Why not?" Parker asked.

After considering the question for several minutes, Pamela said, "Well, I can't honestly think of one reason why not, except…"

"Except?" Parker questioned.

"Except I don't think the uniforms would do much for my figure, with all those bulky guns and things around my waist—uh-uh, not a good look for me," Pamela said.

Both women laughed.

The following morning Parker joined Pamela in the condo kitchen. "You're up early again," Parker said, pouring herself a tall glass of water and sitting down across from Pamela at the counter. "I see that Olivia has joined you. I wondered where she went. She usually follows me around while I have my morning constitutional."

"Oh, I'm sure that my routine was more interesting than yours this morning. It involved treats. She touched noses with Olivia and cooed, "Didn't it, pretty kitty?"

"Pamela," Parker said. "I've never seen you so interactive with Olivia. What's up with that?"

"Well, I've been watching her lately. She really is an interesting little thing—the way she snuggles up to you, begs for petting, watches you, tries to get you to play with her, and those amazing yoga stretches she does. I mean, she has me practically mesmerized. She's quite the little clown and companion. I don't know why it took me so long to discover cats."

"You just weren't paying attention," Parker said. "Cats have been there all along for you to notice and you didn't. Like your newfound passion. You've probably had opportunities to pursue activities like those we were involved in this week, but you didn't."

"Oh, but you're wrong, Par-Par." Pamela said. "I have been involved in things like that, only from the other side, never from the helping side. I've never rescued anyone in my life. I was always too busy keeping my head above water." She grinned. "Yeah, that was invigorating. More, please," she joked.

Parker laughed. "Sooo, Cuz, what are you going to do about it?"

"Huh?" Pamela asked, running her hand over Olivia's fur as the cat slept on the chair next to her. "Well, I stayed up late last night researching, and, do you know what? I think I will consider applying at the police academy. First, I want to maybe do some ride-alongs and spend time talking to police officers while I get my stuff together. Meanwhile, I'll need to support myself. So I'll be job hunting—I mean seriously, for a meaningful job. I know that inside me is a valuable employee, and I'm going to prove that to the world and to myself. You just watch."

Parker stood up and wrapped her arms around her cousin. "I'm proud of you," she said. "I know you can do this."

"Thank you for saying that," Pamela said. "It means a lot, but what I'm most excited about is the pride I feel in myself."

Parker picked up her phone and announced, "It's the detective. Hi, Jud. How are dad and daughter this morning?"

"Wonderful," he said. He laughed. "There are cats in the house already."

"Cats, huh?" Parker said. "Where did they come from?"

"I guess they've always been here. I just didn't notice them, but they came running when Hannah called to them. There are eight cats outside, but the two in the house are Bailey and Priss."

"You sound great," Parker said. "I'm so happy for you."

"Thank you. I'm so thankful to you and your pussycat."

"So what happened after we left yesterday?" Parker asked. "Did you talk to the police officers? Did they take that woman down?"

"I think a cease-and-desist order has been served. There will be an investigation. Once they have transcripts from enough people who were involved, they'll decide what to charge the priestess with—grand larceny, theft, identity theft, grand theft—oh yes, there will be a lot of charges, but it will take time, so Hannah and I are going to get out of Dodge for a while."

"You're leaving?" Parker asked. "Where are you going?"

"We're not sure. There's quite a bit of the country we haven't seen. This seems like a good time to do it—you know, the Grand Canyon, major fishing spots, the tropics, and the Alaskan bush. We want to see it all. Maybe not on this trip, but it's a start."

"That sounds fantastic," Parker said. "I'm so happy for you." She glanced at Pamela as she pulled bacon and eggs from the fridge. "Pamela is talking about joining the police force."

"No kidding?" Jud cheered. "When did she decide that?"

"Maybe last night. She evidently is a natural when it comes to taking down criminals. It got her all twitter-pated."

Pamela made a face and slapped at Parker.

"Good for her," Jud said. "Tell her I'll vouch for her if she needs me to."

"Cool, I sure will," Parker said. She changed the subject, "Did you talk to Felicia or Raif again? Are they all back home and doing okay? Did that wannabe witch ding Doris's bank account?"

"I guess she tried to, but the bankers wouldn't let her make a withdrawal. Those bankers were watching Doris's back."

"Great!" Parker said. "I'm sure her kids are relieved."

"You betcha," Jud said. "So are you staying on, or...?" he asked.

"I think I'll stay and finish the stories that are mounting. If nothing else happens, I should have some quiet time. Actually, I can write just about anywhere, but yes, I like it here. So maybe we can have dinner or something before you and Hannah head out on your adventure."

"Sounds good," he said.

"Hey, Jud, gotta go. I have a call coming in from my agent."

"You have an agent?"

"I sure do," Parker said. "Talk soon. Hello," she said into the phone.

"Parker, how are you?" Angela May said. "I'm loving the pieces you're sending me, only you're lagging a little, girl."

"I know. I've been out gathering material for more stories. I just finished up with a doozy last night, but I'm back at the condo and ready to complete the other pieces I've started."

"No worries, Parker," Angela said. "As a matter of fact, I'd like you to close up shop there and come down to my office here in LA. Something has come up—something rather, well, big. I want you and Olivia to take it on, if you will."

"Parker hesitated, then asked, "Can you give me a hint? I don't relish closing doors until I see and approve of the window that has opened."

"Huh?" Angela muttered. She then said, "Well, tell Olivia it involves cats—disappearing cats under the most unusual circumstances, and the police aren't much interested, so..."

"Oh," Parker said. "Even as worn out as I feel right now, that does sound interesting."

"I thought I could pique your interest," Angela said. "Can you meet me at my office tomorrow at eleven?"

"I'll be there," Parker agreed. She ended the call and looked down at Olivia, who was now standing with her paws on Parker's knees, looking up at her and meowing. "Oh," she said, "you overheard that? Are you up for a new adventure?" She ran her hand over Olivia's fur. "I take that as a yes. Road trip, Olivia! Pack your bags; it sounds like it could be a most fasinating case."

Made in the USA
Coppell, TX
07 February 2022